27 Words

Also by KL Palmer

The Endurants

Writing as
KL Collins

Pipe Dream

27 Words

a novel

KL Palmer

WordCrafts Press

27 Words is a work of fiction. The author has endeavored to be as accurate as possible with regard to the times in which the events of this novel is set. Still, this is a novel, and all references to persons, places, and events are fictitious or are used fictitiously.

27 Words
Copyright © 2017
KL Palmer

Cover concept and design by Mike Parker

ISBN: 978-1-957344-35-5

Published by WordCrafts Press
Cody, Wyoming 82414
www.wordcrafts.net

To my Dad.

Chapter 1

*A*thousand eyes were watching me. Nobody in the room was talking, and the only sound was a muffled cough from the darkness in the back of the auditorium. Why wasn't everyone whispering to their neighbors? Shouldn't they be playing on their cell phones or even sleeping—like normal teenagers?

I quickly thought back to high school when I was sitting where they were today. I couldn't tell you the name of one person that came to speak, nor could I recall one subject matter that he or she would have even talked about. Did we even have guest speakers? Since when did students get so interested in educational assemblies?

I should have been scared. Anyone else would argue that I would have to be. But I've given this speech so many times that I could keep to the strict 17-minute timeslot down to a millisecond. School administrators are warned that if they want their assembly to last longer than that they'd better get a second speaker or fill in the time with their own agenda. I was usually triple-booking schools around an area, so I would check into an office and leave within a 30-minute window on many occasions.

Today was an exception. I only had this one appointment, and I had to drive outside of my normal territory for this particular speaking arrangement. It was nice to be telling my story that morning at the place I grew up—a different scenario from the usual venues within the hustle and bustle of bigger cities. I was speaking in my hometown, Little Lake, Virginia.

The young principal, who not only was new since I was at the school but coincidentally also appeared to be my age, started with introductions on what the subject of the assembly was about and why I was here to speak with them. "Depression doesn't just mean sadness," he poignantly said.

My hands folded in front of me, I looked up at him from his left. Man, was he tall. I listened as he continued.

"It can be a killer. It is important that the students today…"

I was deep in thought wondering how an auditorium could still smell the same 10 years later and how that one scent would always be ingrained in my mind when the clapping that waved across the room startled me back to reality.

I smiled, took a deep breath of that familiar air, and began. "Hello everyone. My name is Lily Calhoun. I was born 27 years ago, here actually. This is my hometown. And today I come back to visit you at this, my alma mater. It's important that you know a few more things about me. They're the reasons I was invited to talk with all of you today."

Exactly 16 minutes and 48 seconds later, I said my thank yous, turned and shook the hand of Principal Albertson, and took my seat on a high stool near the back of the stage. He asked if anyone had any questions for me, and then I immediately felt the nerves creep over my body.

This was the part I dreaded the most. It wasn't that I didn't want to help. Of course I did. If someone had questions, I needed to answer them. This was the time I was most anxious, though, and it came with the *not knowing* of what was next.

I swallowed hard. I was nervous that all eyes were on me and that as a whole we all waited and anticipated the first question to be asked.

It wasn't that I wouldn't know the answers. I knew my story inside and out. I *was* my story. There was nothing that they could ask that would bother me or that I wouldn't know.

A shouted voice came from the back of the room, "So, are you single?"

Nope. I was wrong.

Chapter 2

*A*fter the catcalls settled down, scolding of the young man was done, and the principal redirected the discussion, I breezed through the volley of questioning that followed for the next ten minutes.

As I was walking off stage I faintly heard someone call me damaged goods. "Teenagers," I mumbled. They could be so mean today. I really am glad I wasn't in school now. I thought we had it bad ten years ago. It was never this brutal. I'd gladly take my boring office job over this.

I chuckled to myself as I slid into the driver's seat of my sedan. I looked in the rear-view mirror at my daughter's empty seat and spoke to it like Emmy would be watching and able to hear me, "Well you can tell I'm a mom now, can't you?"

There was, of course, no response. No, she was at daycare, hopefully learning how to *not* act like a teenager today. The clock read 11:02. I needed to get back on the road to pick her up before her three-year-old checkup. I cannot believe it has already been that long since she was born. That was a night I would never forget.

I loved being pregnant. I never got sick, felt fat, or had a swollen or arching body part, but the last week before my due date was a landslide into the other direction. I got the flu, or at least I felt like it. My back hurt, legs hurt worse, and I couldn't tell where my ankles ended and feet began. My face became twice the size of a melon, and my rings became permanent fixtures on my hands. I was miserable. But I continued to work and never once complained. Why would I complain about something as wonderful as bringing life into this world?

My supervisor, Valerie, took one look at me when she saw the changes that happened to me over the weekend and tried to send me home. My due date was the following Sunday, and I argued that I hadn't even hit my nesting stage yet. I was determined to get past this and work until the last minute.

That last minute was about twenty seconds later when my water broke right there in her office on her gray carpet. I was mortified. Val was elated. I don't think she cared one bit about the carpet. She was just excited that she was right in telling me I should have left for the day. It turned out my nesting must have taken place the weekend before, and I missed it with being so sick.

When Emmy was born later that night I didn't care if my body grew another head, and I turned neon orange. I was in love with that little girl, and she became the new light that helped to drive me through life every day.

And now, just a few dozen miles away from holding her again, I was excited to be heading home.

Chapter 3

*M*y phone shrilled from the passenger seat. I pressed the Bluetooth button on my steering wheel and gave my formal hello, "This is Lily speaking. How can I help you?"

"Lily, my darling," Will replied in his best (but very fake) British accent.

I laughed. "Hey honey. Just heading home."

"How'd it go?"

"I think pretty well. They were quiet, so that must mean something." I didn't tell him about the boy's relationship status question.

"Yup. Quiet means good. Means they're listening…at least that's what we hope, right? Hey I'm calling for a couple reasons. One, of course, is to tell you I love you."

I laughed again. "I love you too. What else do you need?"

"I wanted to…" His comments were cut short when his desk phone rang. "Hold that thought. I'll call you right back."

I said good-bye and knew not to be offended for him cutting our conversation short. It came with the job. The moment the desk phone rang someone was in need. More times than not that need was a life or death situation. I hoped it wasn't too desperate for both his and the caller's sake.

Chapter 4

*A*t 24 years old, I was a part-time clerk and full time volunteer for the center when I met the man I would one day call my husband. Will Calhoun was tall, blonde, and extremely good looking—so good-looking that most girls were intimidated by him. They assumed he was married, mean, gay, or a player. He was, in fact, none of the above.

He was, however, burned by his fiancée from a long-term college relationship. She slept with his fraternity brother in the house—more specifically in Will's bed—and then publically vowed to be a better person and never do anything to hurt him again. Two weeks later she broke up with him, through a text message.

His grades suffered. His scholarship was put into jeopardy. To save face he swore off relationships until he settled into an upper management position and established security in his life. That, he thought, should buy him plenty of time.

Apparently, that all fell to the wayside when I came to work at the center. He enjoyed telling the story of his encounter with love at first sight—seeing me walking in slow motion toward him, soft music was playing in the background, and I shot him a shy smile. Every office romance movie wished it was as classic as our meeting.

To be truthful it was a scene from a different movie, more like Jane Fonda in *9 to 5*. I was in the copy room getting memos from the printer when I tripped over the carpet and fell into the tray, and papers started shooting out of the machine with no place to land but the floor. Together we couldn't find the power button, so Will unplugged the machine. He bent to help me up, and we literally bumped heads. I ran off embarrassed and then tripped again, this time over the cord that he had just unplugged. I stumbled over a trash can and then landed face first in the director's office.

Unhurt, except for my ego, I avoided going anywhere for the rest of the week. Will felt bad and brought me coffee and flowers the next morning then Chinese takeout for lunch so I didn't have to leave my cubicle.

We had dinner a few weeks later and soon after his new reputation as a grown version of Little Rascal's He-Man-Women-Hater fizzled. Our simple country wedding took place eight months later under the biggest, blazing-red maple tree on my grandparents' small farm. I wore a simple lace-covered dress with a small train. A wildflower crown encircled my loose bronze curls.

Only our immediate families were there. My dad walked me down the grassy aisle and gave me away with large silent tears running down his cheeks. He didn't think I noticed as he turned away and swiped his face with his sleeve. But I did notice. It was the most cherished moment of the entire day.

Chapter 5

*I*t was about ten minutes later when my phone rang again. I answered, and Will was whistling at me. "Hello my sexy woman," he whispered.

I laughed in response. He was always making me giggle, something that was very important for me and my marriage. One trait I never wanted to lose in a relationship was sense of humor, and we still kept each other laughing.

"I'll be back in town in a little while. Emmy's appointment is at 3:30, and we'll be home after that. Hopefully the shots won't be too bad this time."

"Okay. And that's what I was going to ask before. Want me to stop by and get a pizza on my way home? I'll get pineapple just for my girls," he said in a sing-song voice.

I knew he'd pick every last piece off of his slices, but he always thought of us first. "Works for me. I think I'll stop by and see Dad before I pick up Emmy. I made good time coming back, and I need to see how he's doing."

Will always encouraged me to spend time with Dad. He was in stage-4 kidney failure due to years of having to battle, mostly successful, diabetes. "Enjoy your visit. See you this evening. Love you."

I ended with our signature good-bye. "More than you'll know."

As I turned off the highway on the exit to my father's house, I still had the smile on my face from talking with Will. I loved that man. I never knew I could be so happy, and who I thought would be a fairytale prince charming that I'd marry when I grew up was nowhere near the league this guy was in.

As a young girl I dreamt of the same Cinderella love story that every girl my age did. I knew in my mind that the man I would marry would be gorgeous, of course, and a hard worker, obviously, since I would need to stay at home and raise the three to four babies I'd have.

I remember swaddling and taking turns feeding and changing every last one of those doll babies in my bedroom. When I did work it would be at the local grocery store, because I loved to operate the battery-powered toy cash register I'd gotten for my sixth birthday to rescan the pantry items Mom would bring home each week. I'd take everything out of the brown bags, weigh them, scan them, and re-bag them. Mom didn't care as long as I helped unload the car. I'd come home from the *store* and the cycle of my innocent life would begin all over again.

Now, only part of that fantasy was true. I got the prince charming. Motherhood was a lot harder than passing around plastic silent dolls. I didn't know about colic or reflux when I was pretend feeding them years ago. And another reality I learned is that grocery stores don't pay a lot. They aren't as appealing to the bank account as I had thought that dream job would be. Grocery stores are also not luxurious to shop at. Instead of the fun operation of the register my time was spent on the other side of the counter filling the till with my paycheck. It's even harder having to rush around the place with a screaming child after running out of diapers and formula on the same day.

It became apparent quickly that I would need a two-income household to raise even one baby. I couldn't imagine what it would take for four of them. But those two people in my house were the loves of my life. They were more than I ever could have imagined one day being blessed with. And if it required me to work a cash register, I'd do it in a heartbeat, and I'd love every minute of it.

Maybe that is what is missing from people's lives. Once they grow up, they stress about the finances, outstanding work, and adult issues and forget about the innocence and the fun they had in getting to be where they are today. I probably put at least three hours a day in playing house and working my *job* and never got a penny. Now mind you I probably lost 60% of my youthful energy since then, and I wasn't allowed to fit a nap into my day anymore, but I have come to enjoy my adult life. I think if more people remembered that, they too wouldn't be so grumpy.

Chapter 6

I continued to drive down a country road with about 30 miles to go, headed southeast toward the small town where my dad now lived—the town with only a post office, coincidentally the size of a stamp, a three-stool bar, and of all things a fudge store.

That fudge store was something else. It smelled so good, even with the windows up in the car. The shop was located at the corner where a stop sign made you sit and smell. Sugar seeped through the vents. I had a sweet tooth and stopped every time I came to visit him. I'd buy Dad sugar-free chocolate and me a pound of peanut butter fudge.

The idea of the store made me think of Will and how he kept an old candy dish on his desk. Instead of candy, though, it held three balls—a yellow one, blue one, and red one. They laid peacefully in their place beside his headset until ready for action. As Will sat on the phone talking with hospital personnel, patients, or anonymous callers he would juggle. At first I assume it was out of nervous habit. He said that it *wasn't* nervous but *indeed* a habit. He did it to keep the conversation upbeat. If I ever wondered if he was on a call I'd just look for the balls sailing above the cubicle divider. He's since moved up into an office now, but once in a while a ball will get away from him and roll into the hallway.

I bought him a bag of kisses one year to fill the candy dish. He kept the bag in a drawer and would occasionally fish out a kiss to eat. When I asked why he didn't put the kisses into the candy dish, he looked at me like I had just sprouted a horn from my head and gasped out the words, "That dish is for my juggling balls, not candy."

I didn't say anything—just put the next bag of kisses into the drawer.

He juggled. I, on the other hand, doodled. I had notebooks full of cartoon drawings of people and animals and more elaborate scenery and names penciled like graffiti onto the drawn walls.

Nothing that I created would sell like a Picasso, but it was nervous energy expelled as I walked callers through difficult times. Many of the drawings I made involved people's faces. I would pretend they were the person on the other end of the line. It made the call even more personal to me. There were many sketches left unfinished. The call would end successfully. Those are the ones I cherished the most. Even though mouths were left undone and eyes weren't completely shaded they were complete in their own way.

While we were still just newlyweds, we traveled to churches of every religious affiliation telling stories to the youth congregations. My favorite part was learning about each religion and who the kids were. Will's favorite part was their potluck lunches—the fellowship part, not just the food. I'd sketch pictures of the kids and label them with Bible verses. Will would juggle to keep them entertained while they waited their turn. I giggled thinking how we must have looked like a traveling sideshow. But it was fun. Those were memories I'd carry with me forever.

After Emmy was born we settled down in Mallory, located in north central North Carolina. We bought a house and continued to work for the Hope and Wellness center, but now I did so in a full-time capacity. Will was now director of counselors, and I have become the Marketing Manager and Outreach Liaison.

Our beautiful daughter Emmy had lots of long dark blond curls and blue eyes like her dad. She was as girly as could be on the outside but loved playing with trucks and kicking a ball. Emmy loved digging outside in the dirt as much as she enjoyed playing with dolls and dressing like a princess. She was a very well-rounded little girl and always kept busy and stayed true to the meaning of her name. Emmy, short for *Emmeline*, meant *whole, universal, and hardworking*. At the age of only three she portrayed all of these meanings as deep as her soul.

And she was genuine. As was her namesake, the memorable, effervescent Ms. Emmeline Johnson.

Chapter 7

*D*id I hear someone say something about cardiac arrest? Was I dreaming?

I opened my eyes to see a black nurse tower over my face. She smelled good, like lilacs and cinnamon. The name badge attached to her collar read *Emmeline*. "Welcome back lil' miz sunshine."

Welcome back? I didn't know where I came from or that I even went away. To me I just woke up from an afternoon nap.

The beeping to my left told me I wasn't at home.

Who was Emmeline?

"What is that annoying beeping? Am I at a hospital?" My voice was hoarse, and I croaked.

Emmeline whispered when she talked. She told me I was on the pediatric floor at St. Timothy's Medical Center.

Pediatric floor? Did she just say pediatric? I have no idea why, but I was more upset that they'd put me on the kiddie floor than to tell me why I was in the hospital in the first place. I was 17 years old, technically still a child, yeah, but who told them it was okay to put me here with a bunch of toddlers?

So I asked Emmeline.

"Kory over there's ten. She's not a toddler."

I glanced over and saw a small figure of a young girl sleeping on her side. Kory was tiny for being ten. Dark circles framed under and around her eyes. Even asleep she had a constant wheeze as she breathed.

"Why's she here?" I asked before I even wanted to know about myself, but I probably already knew by that time.

Kory had Cystic Fibrosis, Emmeline explained.

I stared at the little girl and saw a smile start to creep over her lips then. Her eyes flew open, and she yelled, "Gotcha Emmeline! I wasn't sleeping. You thought I was though, didn't you?"

She then fell into a terrible coughing fit causing the nurse to leave my bedside to tend to her. Kory appeared to be a happy kid—tiny, skinny, obviously sick, but happy.

I closed my eyes again.

$\mathcal{M}$y parents woke me up. They were fighting when they walked through the door. Their raised voices forced my eyes to shoot open.

Seeing this they switched to happy Mom and Dad mode and fawned over me, exclaiming how excited they were to see me awake and telling me how scared they were that they thought they lost me. It was typical *Dave and Sharon* behavior. I was not in the mood.

I looked to my left. Kory was sitting up in bed talking to her mom. They exchanged a brief conversation, and her mom hugged her and said she'd be right back and quickly left the room. After her mom shut the door she suddenly turned to me. "So, tell me. Who are you?"

Ignoring my parents, I looked over at her. "My name's Lily. You're Kory, right?"

She nodded quickly and studied me before continuing. "Why are you here? You don't look like us CF patients."

A new nurse had come in and was stopped by my mom, obviously upset at something she did or didn't do. Dad was policing her to make sure she didn't cause a scene, so I instead turned to Kory. "I apparently attempted suicide. Unsuccessfully." Then I mumbled to myself, "Just another thing I'm not good at."

"Apparently? And suicide? Like kill yourself? That's so dumb!" Kory whispered loudly.

My eyes opened wider in shock.

She continued, "I mean I'm just trying to *live* over here, and you're over there trying to *die?* Wanna trade places?"

"What are you talking about?"

"I have CF—cystic fibrosis. They beat my back, make me wear a stupid vest, and even after all that I barely catch my breath—not to mention the thick, yucky stuff they try to break up just so I don't die. So yeah, I can't imagine what would make you wanna end your life."

While my parents continued to talk—mostly argue—with each other and the nurse, I tried to think of what I could possibly say to this girl. Finally, I just had to admit the truth. "Yeah, I'm pretty stupid. Now what do I do?"

Kory shrugged. "I don't know. Stop feeling sorry for yourself? There's more important things to worry about anyway."

"Really? Like what? You're ten. You don't know what problems there are in high school."

"No. I don't. But I know there are tougher things to worry about at this moment. You're making it into a big deal… and for nothin'. Just live. And watch cartoons. Biggest decision of the day should be whether to watch Scooby or Spongebob." Kory rolled her eyes in an exaggerated manner and reached for the tethered remote beside her bed.

Smiling, I said, "I'm gonna like you kid. I'd pick Scobby."

Chapter 9

$\mathcal{M}$om pulled the curtain between me and Kory and took the seat on my left side. Dad fell into the rocker/glider contraption to my right. I looked at him first and then Mom. "So, you must be fighting because of me, huh?"

Mom took my hand, "Why on earth would you think that?"

"Well let's see—your only daughter tried to kill herself, ends up in the hospital from cardiac arrest, is unconscious—I don't have any idea for how long—and the moment you see her alive and awake you're at each other's throats. Isn't rocket science here, folks."

My words reached something in my mom. At first her tight drawn lips and rigid posture said she was angry, and then it quickly melted into a pile of sadness. Her head fell into her hands as she rested on her elbows on her knees. She was deflated.

Dad spoke up, "We're not fighting over what happened to you—we just don't understand what we could have done differently. We wish we could have prevented it."

Not one thing during the entire suicide attempt nor anything leading up to it had anything to do with my parents. At least I couldn't imagine that it did. I was sad. No, I was more than sad at what happened to me at school. I guess if my parents were home they could have seen it on me…in me…but I probably wouldn't have told them anything. No, they wouldn't have been able to see anything differently, or I just would have tried harder to keep my mask of happiness on me.

Chapter 10

*W*ithin the two days Kory and I were together we became closer than some sisters. I would send one of my parents, who couldn't seem to leave me alone if someone paid them to, to get ice cream or magazines, and then she'd send her mom, who was the only person to ever visit her, for fast food, and we'd share our mint chocolate chip and French fries over the latest teen gossip.

She went home that Wednesday, and I was transferred to the mental health floor for an evaluation. It was humiliating and embarrassing, *but necessary*—their words, not mine.

My mom explained that it was protocol and that I should just get through it and then we'd go home. When she wasn't in the room, Dad would say it was important and that they were keeping me so they'd understand what we needed to do as a family to get better. I mentally rolled my eyes. They were still fighting, and they didn't even know it.

So, that was my new home for a while. It kind of made me wish to be back on the pediatric floor, toddlers and all. Instead I had the *Mental Ward, Looney Bin, Nut House, Funny Farm*—there were many names for the psychiatric floor of St. Timothy's Medical Center where I was residing. Patients there, well, those aware enough of their surroundings, always joked about what it should be called.

While in *Crazy Town*, as I called it, I met Holly—age 15. She had an eating disorder—well, *every* eating disorder. She was anorexic, then bulimic, and finally went through a terrible relationship with binge eating. When one didn't give her the results she tried another one.

Holly had also been sneaking her mom's diet pills. Then she

became bold and stole them from the small town pharmacy. The owner, an uncle of hers clued Holly's mom in on what she was doing, and they had an intervention, bringing her to the hospital. They actually saved her life.

By the time she was admitted into the hospital, her hair had already begun to fall out in chunks. She had been wearing hats to cover up her condition. I overheard the doctors tell her mom that she was probably days away from death had she not come in. Her kidneys had stopped functioning and she had the heart of as an 80-year-old.

At first Holly was mad at her family for dragging her there and even more mad at herself for getting caught. But after fighting them and the doctors for a while, she finally gave in and accepted their help. She knew God was there the day she surrendered. She cried for hours, until tears no longer came. Her eyes swelled shut, and she slept for over 16 hours straight. She's been gaining strength ever since.

I only spent a short stint on that floor, but the best advice anyone ever gave me came from that frail girl. She was fighting for her life—another one in as many days to cross my path. She said when she gets out of there she wanted to be an advocate for girls going through what she went through. "Speak up for people who cannot speak for themselves. Protect the rights of all who are helpless," she said.

I thought she was wise beyond her 15 years. Don't get me wrong—she was. She just wasn't the originator of that saying. I later learned that was from Proverbs. But she was the one who pointed me down the path I'm on today. The hospital discharged me before the week was over. They realized I was just dumb girl who made a *very* stupid mistake.

I was mortified at the new rumors that would start at school. I argued with my parents that I couldn't go back. They agreed it might be best to start over, so I cut my hair, streaked it blond, and transferred to the private school in town for my senior year. It would be here that I would sit beside someone for many classes with an unfortunate and familiar name.

Ryan.

He had the same hair color and build as "the other Ryan" but had a last name with a letter off from mine, and in a small school that usually means you're stuck by the same people throughout your entire educational path, even if that path only ran the length of one year.

I stayed to myself as best as I could. I barely spoke. To anyone. But seeing him every day was something I couldn't avoid, and he constantly reminded me of "the other Ryan." So, I changed his name to *Bryan* in my mind. The day I did that kind of made me feel freer—at least I told myself it did.

I also thought about that dumb saying of hindsight being 20/20. Man, that good ol' hindsight would have saved a lot of heartache for me and my family if only it was present when I needed it most back then. But then, the quiet, smart, funny guy that sat in front of me seven classes a day wouldn't continually be salt rubbed into the wound that was "the other Ryan" who had of course been a main player, an accelerator for my quick path to self-destruction.

Chapter 11

*G*rowing up there were two things that our family valued most. They were hard work and my brother Brandon's talent in sports. It sounds corny, I know. And looking back it really was pathetic.

Living in Little Lake, Virginia was pretty much like growing up in the *middle* of the middle of nowhere, if that's even possible. I'd say it was near something for reference, but it really wasn't. The closest hotel to stay in was located across the state line in North Carolina.

While living there in the middle of nowhereland, besides the peace and quiet and lack of city noise, there was also a lack of jobs. My dad took a position with a company that sold energy saving devices. He was a commercial sales manager and would be the one to travel to corporations and businesses demonstrating the latest model of whatever machine they had at that moment. I really didn't know what the contraptions did, but my mom was happy each month the electric bill came in, and it was less than they thought it would be. So at least the devices worked.

Anyway, Dad's job took him away—a lot. He was frequently gone the entire week every time he traveled. That meant he'd only get to be home late Friday night through Sunday afternoon. Sometimes, when he was traveling to the West Coast, he wouldn't get back until Saturday morning.

Mom stayed at home and dabbled in coupon collecting. My job was to go through her envelopes and books of cut out coupons and find those with the expiration dates that had passed. I realized I threw away a lot more than we kept, so I don't think that hobby was one that worked that well.

Another of Mom's jobs was to play the part of the missing parent, so with Dad away she filled his shoes by doing the normal manly jobs of trash run, mowing the grass, and pressure washing the fence when needed. She also was the taxi for all of Brandon's practices and tournaments. I will admit he was an extremely talented soccer player. We all knew he was going far.

Mom molded him as a man and prepped him for college. They completed paperwork for scholarships and worked with athletic directors at the schools he wished to attend. Most weekends were spent traveling the tri-state area for soccer games. He never missed one. And on most occasions, I didn't either.

I'd be there with Mom in the stands. Dad would be just coming back from a trip or preparing for another one, but on some occasions we were all together watching him play. I loved those trips. Mom would be so engaged in keeping track of Brandon's stats and videotaping for him to review for improvements that I was usually there by myself, but when Dad came we'd spend a lot of time going back and forth to the concession stands or watching parents and other spectators, trying to figure out who their kids were that they were rooting for.

Around the spring of my sophomore year, I volunteered in the town library a few nights a week and on some Saturdays, so it was my new excuse to stay home—especially when Dad was coming back from work. I guess with the word *volunteer* in your title you could get out of being there to support your brother, but by that time I really was starting to get over it, over the whole soccer thing.

So it was during one of those weekends when I caught Whitney by the bleachers with Ryan—yeah, that "other Ryan" from my first school. Mom was gone out of town with Brandon, and Dad was scheduled to come home that Friday. On his way back he was supposed to pick me up, but because he was late from work, I ended up in the wrong place at the wrong time.

Chapter 12

*W*hat started as them arguing in the hospital had turned into full out screaming when I left Crazy Town. I know there were a few weeks that the fight had time to brew, but I was shocked that it had gotten this bad.

Dad blamed Mom for never paying attention to their daughter while babying their practically grown son by refusing to let him go out of town on trips without her. Mom fought back with, *at least she stayed home with the kids.* Dad reminded her of being with Brandon most of the time and not seeing my issues until it was too late. Mom accused him of never being home when there were *other jobs out there.*

We all knew deep down that probably wasn't true.

Neither one fought fair, but I knew Dad was only trying to make a living, and Mom was just trying to help Brandon get to college. Neither was wrong. Both weren't right, either.

Eventually, Dad gave in and sacrificed his career and his salary. He took a position at the small used car lot as the finance manager. Mom went back to work in the bakery of the supermarket in the next town over the summer Brandon graduated from high school. It was the same time I transferred schools as well. We were all starting fresh.

And it worked.

Well it worked for a few years.

By my junior year in college my mom admitted she should have been there more for me. She started to wonder if she was the problem and decided instead of trying to fix that problem, the best thing for all of us was for her to move out.

Dad didn't stop her.

He didn't fix it either.

That was the year I realized he needed to be fixed himself. He admitted that he was secretly fighting diabetes for the past decade. Nobody knew it besides him and his doctor.

Chapter 13

*D*ad was walking back from the mailbox when I approached his narrow driveway. He lived in a small duplex on the edge of town. He stopped on the sidewalk and smiled in my direction. His happiness was apparent. I smiled back and pulled into the driveway, stopping a few feet behind his once black late 80s model pickup truck. He lived a modest life, still putting in many hours a week at the car dealership.

"My Lily girl! What brings you by today?" He knew I worked every day at the center, so he was surprised to see me.

I didn't want to tell him I was at Little Lake. I guess I didn't want to bring back any bad memories for him. So I got out of my car and hugged him before quickly answering, "Just coming back from a school over the Virginia Line. I have a little bit of time before picking Emmy up—thought I'd stop in and check on you."

"Check on me? Why? Am I changing or something?" he asked sarcastically.

We walked together toward the house. "Are you taking your medication?"

"Yes."

"Are you telling me the truth?" I stopped a step ahead and looked back at him.

He nodded then replied, "I said yes."

"I'll just have to ask Maggie." Maggie was actually Margaret Pruett the woman that Dad had been dating for the past two years. She lost her husband six years before and had two grown sons, Eric and Eli. Eli was a senior in college, and Eric was married with an

18-month-old daughter. They lived in the same small town as their mother. This was also the same small, fudge-shop town as my dad.

Dad and Maggie were not as serious as I had encouraged, but she was good for him. She kept him fed, medicated, punctual for doctor appointments, and most importantly, back in the church.

"She'll tell you the same thing. You have her trained well."

"Good. I need to keep you around for a while. I understand you'd like to see what's on the other side, but I'd like you to stay over here with us for a while."

After we got inside, I poured a glass of water from the pitcher in the refrigerator and motioned with my drink, asking if Dad wanted one. He nodded, and I handed him the already full glass and grabbed another from the cabinet for myself. As I poured it he asked about the assembly I just came from. I still didn't tell him where I went, but we laughed about the boy's question, and I told him how I felt like it was the one part of my job that I loved the most.

"Really? I never saw you as the speaker type," he commented.

"No, I certainly don't like speaking in public, but where else do you have the full—okay, *mostly* full—attention of hundreds of kids at one time. Commercials and videos couldn't emotionally touch a fraction of the same group of kids. I just hope it touches the right people at the moments that they need it the most."

"You're changing them. You don't need to see the immediate proof to know it. One day they will remember you. Might not even be for themselves. Their kids might need your message, and it comes back around years from now."

I drank down my water and then a laugh caught my lips. "Dad, that's why I love you… you're always… have always been the shining light in my life."

The first speech I ever gave, aside from the two-minute assignments given in English class, was on the day of my high school graduation. I wasn't picked as valedictorian—wasn't even sure if I was in the top half of my class—but I asked to give the speech. At first Principal Wilson said it would be too depressing. The irony there, I know. Then he backpedaled, apologized for being rude, and accepted my offer since nobody else volunteered.

What I planned to say had to be approved by the principal. Of course everything I wrote down and turned in was rejected. Principal Wilson said it was too dark and that what I needed to say should be uplifting and encouraging. I looked him in the eyes and leaned on the desk and said, "What is more encouraging and uplifting to a lost soul than to see a survivor standing before them?"

Before he could argue with doubts about anyone being lost, I continued, "You think the students all know what's ahead? None of them do. They're scared. They may have scholarships or plan on joining the workforce, but they, along with everyone in between, don't know what to expect and certainly not what's ahead for them. What about the parents? Don't you think they're scared?"

He just looked at me. "That is what I will be talking about. Not just about a lost girl. I'm gonna tell about how the girl was found and how there is a light—no matter how dim it might be—at the other end of the tunnel."

And so he agreed, signed off on the speech, and allowed me to go ahead with my message.

Many people at graduation didn't know my situation. I only

told a handful of people I eventually got close to. Faces of shock had fallen around the stage, and I smiled. Before today I doubted anyone would have talked to me after graduation anyway. Now I knew for certain they wouldn't.

After my speech—which I thought was anything but dark—and before I left the podium, I needed to say one last thing. I felt that I was encouraged to dedicate my recovery to my dad. I don't know why God directed me to only dedicate it to him and not my mom too. Maybe it was because God knew Dad was sick even though he wouldn't admit it to anyone. I still wasn't sure how I felt about how Dad had reacted to my issues, but I knew I was meant to simply give him a message. It came to me in just 27 words—again. And I had written it on the same Post-it I wrote my potential suicide note on.

Dark? Yes. Sad? Maybe. Ironic? No.

I thought it was the right thing to do at the time. This time I wrote on the back: "I love you, Dad. Please know that. Thank you for saving my life. We'll never stop fighting this war, and we'll win. Never surrender. Your Daughter, Lily."

Chapter 15

I remembered every word as if it was yesterday, but still that note stays hung up at work, the side dedicated to my dad facing out for all to see.

I could tell by looking at their faces that my dad was proud, but my mom's faced showed something else. She was actually jealous. She couldn't believe I had directed everything to him and not her since she was there for me too, more in fact because she stayed home and didn't work *all over God's green earth* as she'd say. I believe that dedication, though, is what set her off, pushing her over the edge.

The next day she apologized for acting as she did. She said she was proud of me too and was *amazed at my recovery*. Yes, those were her exact words. Sometimes I wondered if she even thought about what she said before saying it.

I didn't think things between Mom and Dad ever really got better, but they didn't get worse. They didn't fight, but they really didn't talk either. I would come home from work, and they would be in separate rooms. Sometimes Mom was watching television, and Dad was in the garage; or he'd be in the living room, and she'd be doing laundry or in the kitchen. It probably looked harmless to some but to not have been in the house together for as long as Dad worked out of town they should have been catching up on lost time. Instead they were avoiding each other while in the same house.

As soon as Mom filed for divorce, she moved to Tennessee. She said it was to be closer to her parents who lived in Knoxville along with her brother and his family, but we knew it was partly to be away from us. And nobody was surprised when it happened. Today when I think about it, I definitely wasn't surprised—but I was angry; angry that I fought to not give up, and she just gave up and walked away as if it was any other Tuesday.

Chapter 16

"Brandon came by last week."

I looked up at Dad and simply nodded twice—slowly. Brandon really had not been around since Mom moved away. He lived near Wilmington, close to the coast of North Carolina, about a five-minute drive from Wrightsville Beach. He wasn't married, although he'd been dating the same girl, Cassidy, since college. She was from a rather wealthy family. I felt like she was the reason for him staying away. Brandon wouldn't admit it, but it was a feeling that I got when he did actually come around.

We only met Cassidy three times, and two were by accident when we ran into them when they were visiting her family in Greensboro. They said they were in love. Brandon said it more times than we needed to hear, but since he was my brother I believed him, and I was happy for him. I just wished I saw him more. I also wish he understood that times were different back then, and I wanted to be able to one day explain everything to him.

"He told me that he and Cassidy are getting married."

My eyes grew wide. I knew it shouldn't have come as a shock to me, but something still bothered me, nonetheless. The relationship was over seven years in the making. They must be compatible, or it wouldn't last this long.

"When?"

"They don't know. She wants it to be sometime next summer," Dad said.

"Why wait until then? I mean seven years of dating and now she needs over a year of an engagement. She must need him to save for a bigger ring."

"Lily!"

"I'm sorry. I just miss having him around. Even though he was always traveling with soccer he was still here. Then when Mom left, I thought he'd surely come back and live here at least closer to her too. Instead he moved to the other side of the state."

He shrugged. "I don't know what to tell you Lily girl. I hope he knows how we feel. All we can do is tell him."

"He blames me, Dad."

"He shouldn't"

"Well he does. If I didn't… well, if I wasn't in the hospital, Mom would still be here. He'd still be around."

"It's not your fault. And your mom, well—who knew what else would have set her off. He's a big boy. He knows what's best for him. And who's to say he still wouldn't have gotten with Cassidy, and she'd still have him living over there.

I washed the dishes for Dad and picked up around the house quickly dusting when he wasn't looking and organizing shelves as I did the light cleaning. Dad told me to stop, and as usual I didn't listen. I knew Maggie would take care of him, and she did a lot of the housekeeping. With just one person living there he didn't make a lot of dirty dishes, laundry, or mess around the house. I still felt the need to help. It kept my mind off Brandon and Mom, and I knew he needed to relax.

My phone vibrated in my pocket as I was wiping the kitchen counter. It was Will. "How's it going?" the text read.

I quickly typed, "Good. Leaving here in about 20."

It would get me to the daycare a little after 3:00. The doctor's office was only two blocks from the center. Will knew Brandon distanced himself from us, which meant that my visits with Dad were even more important. We only lived 15 minutes from him, but it was still too far for me. I felt like I was trying to make up for lost time, but his time was running out. I tried not to think about it, but it was inevitable. It was not fair that Dad had taken years away from his family by keeping secrets about his health from us—but I guess we all kept secrets from one another, lasting secrets that might be forever hurtful to the entire family.

I sat down at the table and pulled on my dress boots. Fighting with the zipper, I stopped feeling the need to look up at the man across from me and confessed. "Dad, I have to tell you something."

The look I had must have told Dad I wasn't about to spring a pregnancy or lottery win on him. It was serious. He sat down across the table from me.

"I want to admit something to you that I probably should have said a long time ago. I feel like I spent most of my formative years thinking you didn't like me."

"That's crazy!" he said, but I kept talking so he didn't argue.

"I knew that you *loved* me, of course, but I was never sure you actually, well, *liked* me—as least not as much as you did Brandon."

"Why would you think that?"

"When you *were* home, it was always on Brandon's time. It was his games or practices you attended—even if it was just passing a ball around in the yard, you were together. We never spent time together doing, well, anything that was just the two of us."

"I would have. I guess I should have. And of course I loved you. And liked you." He fought to not roll his eyes at the crazy idea. "There was never any question in my mind."

"I know. Well, I know that now that I'm an adult. Teenage Lily would have liked to have understood that too."

Dad slowly nodded, taking a few seconds to think about what to say next, then spoke. "Do you know how heartbroken I was when you were in the hospital—when everything happened? I was so scared that I could have lost you. I was even more afraid when you came home."

"More afraid?" I asked.

"Yeah, like afraid I'd break you, or something would happen, and you'd break again. Or maybe even you might break me."

"I don't understand. How could *I* break *you?*"

"Can you imagine Emmy hurting? I mean *really* hurting… and you could have done something to prevent it but didn't. Think about it. You'd be devastated. Any parent would be broken over it, fractured by it." He paused, thinking of what more he could say to explain. "Getting involved again or even close to the situation could cause that parent to shatter. Sometimes pulling away makes it easier to pretend everything's fine…" He trailed off and looked as if he had more to say but couldn't find the right words.

I thought telling him my feelings would make me feel better. Instead, it gave me more to think about. I was relieved when my watch told me it was time to pickup Emmy for her appointment. I gave Dad a long hug and whispered that I loved him. I promised to call soon and reminded him, as I always did, to take his medication and eat something.

He laughed, as he always did, knowing that Maggie cooked more food for him each day than a crew aboard a sailing vessel could eat in a week. "Love you, Lily girl," he said shutting the door behind me.

Chapter 17

$\mathcal{M}$om had a boyfriend—at least a *good friend* that was male—before she left Dad, even before I did what I did. I don't know if Dad knew. I've never told him, and I wasn't going to now, but it hurt me that I kept Mom's secret from him, not that I knew if it was even still a secret.

His name was Franklin. I didn't even know that was anything but a last name when I was younger, so I was always waiting for him to say his first name, but he never did. I saw him more often than I liked. At first it was coincidental run-ins while we waited for Brandon's soccer practice to end. His son, Alec, also played on the team.

I never saw them kiss or even hug. He high-fived her once when Brandon hit his third goal of the practice, and they shook hands twice that I know of, but if there was more than a friendship my mom fought hard to hide it, and she did so very well.

I remember he called at least once that I heard. I answered the phone, a man asked for Mom, and I handed her the phone. She mentioned his name, and they laughed, and the call was over quickly. When she hung up and saw me looking at her, she quickly explained that she was confirming when the caravan was leaving for the tournament the following weekend, and I believed her. There wasn't much reason not to.

But the adoring look he gave her had also been etched in my brain. It's the same look Will gives me when he sees me in a tight-fitting dress or when I parade around showing off new heels. It was a longing for more, or what was to come. It's something that until I found love with Will I didn't know about, that I didn't remember witnessing.

I think that look is what confirmed that I didn't need to see anything more to believe it. Mom and Franklin had more than a friendship. With Dad being out of town all the time, she found interest in another man. That same man was available to her, maybe even traveled out of town with the soccer team as well. It's probably on those trips that they fell for each other, probably into each other's arms.

I shook my head. I didn't want to think about that now. Anyway, Franklin still lived in the area, so it wasn't like she moved to Tennessee to run away with him. I know because I confirmed his address on the internet. It's also funny, but based on his social media account he's been happily married for 32 years. Oh, and Franklin really is his first name. I confirmed that as well.

Chapter 18

*I*t was a week since the last assembly that I'd given. I usually liked to hit a few schools a day or at least a couple a week but the fundraising gala plans that I was in charge of for the center were coming together quickly, and I wanted to keep up with them while things seemed to be heading in the right direction.

Today's assembly was at Laurel Mountain High School in a northwestern mountainous area of North Carolina. It was one of the largest schools I'd spoken at in a while. There would be about 800 students at the school, all freshmen through seniors. It was only about a 15-minute drive up the interstate, but for some reason I just couldn't get there today. I could not believe traffic was so bad. I sat completely still for 21, no, now 22 minutes.

With it being the only assembly on the schedule that day, I tried to leave early. I always liked to leave early if possible, even if that means sitting in my car collecting my thoughts or spending time visiting with the office staff. I tend to get a lot of vital information out to the most unsuspecting people during those information talks; a little piece of advice on what to look for or types of comments to listen for have been known to save lives.

June Pritchard was one lady I thought of often. She was the attendance clerk for Washington Heights Middle School near Hillsborough. I was over two hours early for an assembly at that school. I thought it was to be at 11:00 but misread my note. I was actually 1:00. So as I waited around the main office, June asked me if I wanted to grab a bite to eat at the cafeteria. I was starving. Funny how you don't realize you are hungry until smells begin to waft around you. Unfortunately the smells on that occasion included dinosaur-shaped fish nuggets, which was what was on the menu that day.

"I think they ran out of the big kid stick shapes," June said as she stabbed a dinosaur with her fork and flashed her kill in my direction.

"I think you're right," I laughed.

After picking at my food, mostly eating the breading off the fish-o-saurs, I asked her how she liked working at the school.

She swallowed before answering. "Oh, I love it. You'd think calling parents to tell them their kids are skipping and collecting forged parent's excuses would get boring—but it's the other kids, the good ones, those who are there every day, even if unhappy about it, that make the job worthwhile."

I sipped from my miniature milk carton and then spoke. "I remember when I was in school I was one of those dedicated to come to school even if I was sick."

June nodded her head, "Me too, but could you imagine coming to school every day just to get away from your family."

I looked up at her and blinked. I waited for her to continue.

"It's more common than you think. Whether someone at home is mean, or missing, or there isn't food there but they know they can get a meal or two here… It's just… It's sad."

"And those are the ones that can't participate in after school events to keep them involved here either, right?"

She nodded. "Exactly. No money, parents won't sign for permission, you name it I've heard it."

It was then that I told her my story.

Chapter 19

I wasn't overweight, or too skinny. I dressed okay. I think I talked okay. I was friends with everyone. This was actually probably the reason the teasing first began.

One of my best friends while growing up was Jarrod. Even though we didn't hang out much after school and lived too far from each other to do things on weekends we spent a lot of lunches and study halls catching up with each other.

Jarrod liked to design fashion and write romance fiction short stories. He never had a girlfriend, and I was one of the few females to be around him at all. He never let their comments bother him. He would come back with the wittiest retaliation that left those preying speechless.

So they would come after me. I was not as strong as him. I would go between questioning my friendship with Jarrod to questioning my self-worth. It seems ridiculous now; but back then I didn't know both could play in the same arena together. So I held in my feelings.

This led to a poor decision in relationships—Ty Shipman.

I'd seen the movies. I'd read the books. I knew the handsome star quarterback always ends up with the pretty blonde cheerleader captain. It's the way nature is designed. The Happily Ever After— well, someone's Happily Ever After—certainly not mine. I wasn't blonde, nor was I a cheerleader.

On the other hand, I have also seen the cheesy teen films with the ugly duckling—or just average, awkward girl—getting a makeover and walking arm in arm to the prom with that same quarterback only to later find out it was all trickery.

I never got said make-over, but I was an awkward, average

teenage girl. So whether I was blind to the whole *too good to be true* mantra or even the idea of *the boy's out of your league,* the unfortunate demise of my virginity came by way of Ty losing a bet to the other football players. They said he couldn't steal Lily from the grasp of Queen Jarrod—but he showed them he could. It only took him one sophomore-year homecoming dance, two slices of pizza, a few false promises, a handful of compliments laced with minimal attention, and a four-pack of berry wine coolers.

When I was with him that night, in a broken down ford pickup in his dad's field, I didn't care what got me there. I didn't think about the alcohol or the promises—false or otherwise—didn't remember the past nor think about the future. I was with Ty. My Ty. My prize. I had finally gotten him. My life couldn't be more perfect than it was at that minute. And if the world ended I would have felt nothing but complete.

I shook my head as I thought about it now. I was so wrong back then. I know I shouldn't think it, but I was an idiot. That was actually was I was. A bona-fide idiot. I was an absolute, boy-crazed, desperate, hormone-blinded, pathetic idiot.

That led to the third and final piece of my story—Whitney Lowe. Yes—that same Whitney. She would be my free, now fully-punched ticket to ride aboard the Crazy Train.

Whitney Lowe should be a politician. If she wanted to, she could use the power of her persuasion to obtain world peace once and for all. Instead, her career aspirations turned into a position at the Kuttin' Hutt as a part-time stylist, but before that dream would come true she'd use her influence and energies to aim toward a different mission—to make my life absolutely miserable for the next six months.

Chapter 20

To say Whitney *liked* Ty was a complete and astronomical understatement. Whitney *adored* Ty. She *idolized* him, *worshiped* him, and truly believed in her heart of hearts that she *deserved* him. She was, after all, the blonde cheerleader that was meant to end up with him—happily ever after and everything. But Ty didn't like her. In fact, Ty loathed her. At first he *tried* to date her our freshman year. He, too, knew the quarterback was supposed to date the cheerleader, but her sociopathic tendencies made him defy that stereotype, and he quickly planned to break it off with her. He said she was bossy. We all knew she was actually crazy, if not certifiable then definitely socially verified. Which, if you asked anyone in private, they'd agree that she was. To her face? Never. People valued their lives.

And in any relationship, especially one with Ty, only one man was in charge. And it wasn't her. So she did what any potential dumpee would do, she broke up with him first and started dating the rival team's quarterback by the following weekend. Then, when that guy didn't pay attention to her, and Ty wouldn't take her back, she ran his name through the mud. She would bring him down, reputation first.

But that didn't work. So she slept with his best friend, Kyle. That is what finally caught his attention. He couldn't concentrate on the game knowing his teammate, his best friend could do that to him. He ended the freshman season with a fractured arm and a shattered spirit.

That summer Whitney apologized, swore she had changed and before the next year began they were an official item once again. Not only were they *a* couple but *the* power couple, the one to be like or be afraid of. And I didn't care. I was just beginning to forget the awful situation I had faced with Ty. I almost could look him in the face without wanting to throw up or punch him. Whitney could have him. Good luck… well, to the both of them.

All was perfect in Ty-Whit Land until the night of the homecoming dance. That was the night that Whitney was caught with her skirt up behind the baseball bleachers.

We all know how the story goes. It wasn't Ty she was in lip-locked heaven with. It was *the other Ryan.*

Who caught them?

Me.

Ty and Whitney broke up. Whitney claimed it all happened the same night. Ty made her mad at the dance. She found someone who promised to help her get over him. Ryan stood back and didn't know which direction to run. He didn't deny nor agree with anything he was accused of. I think he was just proud to say he could admit to groping Whitney's backside.

Any way you slice it, if the break-up of the century did happen that night, and it was because of Ryan and Whitney's make-out session. It wasn't from me saying anything to anybody. But you could have fooled me. The way people looked at me the next day, you'd think I immediately went from rooftop to rooftop shouting their indiscretions through a bullhorn. Eyes cut in my direction, and whispers floated around the hallway.

I never said a word. I may have silently celebrated inside thinking that maybe someday I'd use it as black mail, but that ammunition had yet to be loaded. That day you wouldn't know it by everyone at school. It was like a different place to me, almost like I was still dreaming or that I stepped into the wrong school.

I suppose I should have understood what came next was simply Whitney painting herself in the best light. Any rumors she spread about me, including what happened with Ty, only made her look like a star, or the queen, or a hurt and sad wounded flower. Any situation she gave and any lie she said was simply to better herself among her people. I said it before. I was simply in the wrong place at the wrong time. The unluckiest of events unfolded in a very short amount of time. It began with a sequence of misfortunes that fateful night in October: My dad getting stuck at work that night; me having to walk home; choosing the route by the baseball fields; catching the most scandalous act of unfaithfulness of high school history.

It would end with a lot worse.

Chapter 21

*J*une held both hands around her coffee mug. She was finishing a bite of the apple crisp, the one thing that actually looked appetizing on the tray. After taking a long sip, she asked, "So, it's not the normal school cat fight that brings you to schools though, is it?"

I shook my head and leaned onto the table edge with my elbows before continuing.

I never thought anyone could have such power over people. I was taught growing up to listen to authority but to also have a mind of your own. I couldn't understand how everyone else didn't get that same lecture at home. It was like lemmings popped up around me over night.

By homeroom people closest to me stopped talking *to* me and instead talked *about* me. The whispers. The laughing. How did it happen so fast? It buzzed in my mind all day and into my sleep. My mom would ask how my day went. But I couldn't find anything that hadn't been smothered by Whitney's gossip to tell her. I began to give the *fine* and *everything's good* comments. Before, if she asked, I would have listed everything memorable. I wonder now why that wasn't a sign for her to worry about me?

All of that torture went on for exactly three weeks and four days. It also grew progressively worse by the hour, and I found myself measuring it by the minute. The final tick on my explosive timer happened as I was leaving school one Thursday. I usually ducked out and avoided eye contact and crowds. I learned to keep my headphones on at all times even when I wasn't listening to music. It drowned out the cat calls, laughs, and name calling that became too familiar.

That afternoon, though, I felt a hand grab my forearm as a walked outside and down the side steps—that was another change I'd made to my schedule. To avoid the crowds, I'd take the side door. It also conveniently faced the street I'd walk down. I was jerked around the railing and stood face-to-face with Ty.

He pulled me into the shadows of the stairwell and slammed me up against the wall. With his body pressed tight against mine he forced a hard kiss onto my lips causing my teeth to bite down and through my lip. Blood poured into my mouth, and before I could scream his hand was over my lips, tight around my jaw.

He roughly grabbed my chest with his free hand and whispered into my ear that the next time he got his hands on me it would be for more than a cheap feel. He ground himself into me and promised the next time we were together he'd make me beg for it, and then beg more to stop. He warned that my mouth needed to be occupied so I wouldn't run it anymore and that by the time he was done I'd be ruined, and no guy would ever want me. I'd have to be stuck with Queen Jarrod forever. Then as quickly as it began he pulled me from the wall and shoved me into the crowd as they exited down the steps. At the same time he turned left and rounded the building.

I covered my mouth with my left hand and used the sleeve of my shirt to wipe away the hot tears that poured from my eyes. I ran home. I couldn't get there fast enough. But I knew what I needed to do once I arrived. I was going to kill myself. Then he'd never get to put his hands on me again.

June had long since stopped eating. She was staring at me with her mouth open in surprise.

When you write a suicide note, it's the last thing you want to have to think about. By the time the note's due, you just want it to be over. I felt like I had to write something. I had to let my family know I loved them and give my parents peace in knowing why I did what I was going to do.

So I used a Post-it—actually one I was starting to doodle on and had discarded in the trash can. Everything I had to tell them fit on a pale yellow piece of paper that was 3" by 3" in size—27 words in total.

It read, "I love you guys. Please know that. But I'm tired of this life. I'm tired of fighting a war I can't win. I surrender. Forever Yours, Lily."

I was able to recite it by heart. I even dreamt about it at night.

"That, Ms. Pritchard, is why I'm here today." I explained how bullying was the final push that toppled me over the edge, but a buildup of other issues was what brought me to that cliff. Something as unassuming as taking advantage of the free lunch might be the spark that detonates the internal explosion for that child."

June's eyes widened, and as if reading her mind, I knew she was mentally going through the list of students that fit that mold.

"How do you reach out to them?"

"Having me here is a great resource. It's a way to touch people without pulling them aside, calling them out. As I share my story and tell the message, I watch eyes tear up around the crowd, smiles appear, and the light bulbs go off. I know I've reached them. They allowed me in without even knowing." My eyes fell to my plate, and then I continued. "I only ask that those in positions like yours be there to talk when they need you."

She reached across the table and squeezed my hand, accepting the role.

That was a year ago. Now, less than two miles from my destination I can't seem to get to, I'm hoping that I won't miss the next assembly. I'm hoping to be able to help the next group of kids, possibly even save another life.

Chapter 22

With just minutes to spare, I made it. I ran into the principal's assistant and after signing in at the office was quickly shuffled to backstage. I heard kids filing in trying to find seats, and directions given to them to quiet down.

Dr. Martinelli was the principal at Laurel Mountain High School. He was a short, heavy-set man with a crown of gray curls framing his shiny bald head. His little round-rimmed glasses appeared to be a permanent part of the bridge of his nose, and his cheeks held an eternal rosiness. He stood at the podium barely able to reach the microphone. Adjusting it twice to suit his height, he welcomed everyone for being in attendance. There were the usual chuckles and snide comments about being forced too. As if immune to the outbursts, he continued.

"This is Ms. Lily Calhoun. She is here representing the Hope and Wellness Center out of Greensboro." He motioned to his left where I was once again perched high on a stool as if on display. I nodded and smiled waiting for him to continue.

He began the script I had offered him upon my arrival at the school. It was a brief summary of what the Hope and Wellness Organization was about, who we represented, and what our purpose was. His short speech ended with a perfect transition into my story. As he finished, he introduced me again and stepped back from the podium.

Clapping continued as I thanked everyone for having me there. I explained who I was and where I was from trying not to copy what their principal had already told them. I wanted to keep as much of their attention for as long as I could. I went through a brief explanation of my life pre, during, and post suicide attempt. There were a lot of shocked expressions as I described the horror I felt and saw, and then the audience chuckled as I told my stories of Kory and Holly and how friends come in all shapes, sizes, ages, colors, and with any number of personal issues. I explained that my situation and what I went through didn't stop me from being a thriving, loving person today.

Even though I took the boring road to college, I still went. What I didn't tell the kids was that I honestly didn't want to worry about asking anyone to help me pay for it. I knew my parents were burnt out from having to deal with Brandon's road to success and were still paying the hospital for my stupidity, so I applied at the local four-year community college to study business—just plain, old business. I liked accounting and management and knew I could use the degree just about anyway.

I mentioned that two-thirds of the way through college I remembered my conversation with Holly, and I added some social sciences classes to the mix. I also began volunteering at the student helpline at the school. The helpline was designed so a student with any need could call in, and with a few menu selections he or she could be directed to a volunteer who specialized in that issue.

As sad as my depression line should have been, I was one of the busiest resources and also most successful with calls. I loved that position and didn't mind that I didn't get paid. I was needed, and I knew where I wanted to go with my life.

At graduation I ended up with my Bachelor of Business Administration degree with a minor in Sociology. I soon began work at the Hope and Wellness center for depression and grief as a counselor. It was there that I met my husband William Allen Calhoun and I was beginning to live my Happily Ever after.

Chapter 23

*A*round of applause waved across the room, and I took my seat back on the stool. Mr. Martinelli approached the podium one more time, readjusting the microphone for his small statue, and asked if anyone had any meaningful questions.

I smiled thinking of the last time that was asked. As was normal in most cases, though, not a word was spoken nor was a hand raised.

"Okay then, if nobody has anything, I would like to ask our Guidance Counselor Ms. Leonard to come up to talk briefly about a new anti-bullying initiative we would like to implement at our school."

What happened next was illusory—at least it seemed so at the time. It's best described by accounting for what I *do* know. Mr. Martinelli took a couple of steps back to allow Ms. Leonard to pass him to take the podium. He was still to my right by at least ten feet. My perch was around three feet from the side of the stage. Everyone in the auditorium began to clap. Eight hundred sets of hands welcomed her, and I started to stand to applaud as well.

Somewhere around the same time the right-side front door—which led under the stage to an area where a trap door might go—burst open, and a young man's voice told everyone to stay where they were. Something caught my eye to my left, and another man, dressed completely in black, emerged and fired a shot from his gun.

Chaos ensued. People were crying out in confusion and pain. There were students running, falling, and blood curdling screams echoing off the wall. Shots continued to be fired, and the smell of spent ammunition filled the air.

Mr. Martinelli now ran in my direction knocking me and the

stool to the ground as he dove for the shooter. In the process the young man on the right side fired as well. Screaming continued to reverberate around the room.

I flew two feet backward toward the left. My ankle caught in the bottom rung of the stool which tumbled with me to the floor. My shoulder slammed onto the wooden stage. With the principal wresting the shooter to the ground, I knew I needed to get out of there and find help.

Untangling myself from the stool, I drug myself behind the curtain and crawled off the side of the stage. Immediately the darkness opened to a lit hallway, and I froze not knowing where I was or who might be around. Emmy and Will flashed in my mind for a brief second before I knew I had to survive this for them.

Continual muffled screams, bangs, and slamming continued behind me, but nobody was coming down the hall, and I hurried into the first open door I saw. It was a dark, closet-like room, but it was away from the madness and a place for me to think. Pulling myself across the threshold, I slowly shut the door in silence, not even breathing for fear someone would hear me.

When the door was firmly closed, I finally shut my eyes and let out a deep breath, willing my heart to calm.

I laid my head again the door shaking from anxiety. To my right came the biggest surprise of the day, the metal of a pistol flashed in the stream of light from the hallway, and I heard a raspy voice whisper, "You shouldn't be here."

Chapter 24

I gasped, my eyes widened in horror, and I froze in place.

The boy attached to the voice sat forward, leaning out of the darkness of the corner. He was so young. And scared. So many thoughts swirled around in my mind, but nothing came forward, and my voice remained muted.

As if he realized he was holding a gun he tensed up and threw it down. Shaking his head back and forth violently, placed his hands on either side of it to stop the movement and rested his elbows on his knees. Then he sobbed. Each second his sobbing grew louder.

I threw my finger to my lips and shushed him. "You can't be loud. They're… they… they'll hear you out there.

He looked up at me, his tormented face covered in tears and phlegm. He was a mess, but his eyes told his secret. I looked across the room at the gun. And before I could say it, he confirmed my thought. "I was supposed to be out there. I was supposed to do it."

I instantly forgot about the pain in my ankle and the bruise on my shoulder. I moved toward him and settled at his side. Without thinking, I wrapped my arms around his little frame. He accepted my hug but only after rigidly tensing at the foreign gesture of a total stranger. I kept my eye on the gun as I did so. I knew I needed him to talk to redirect his focus.

I gulped and found finally found my voice. "What were you supposed to do?"

"Bryce said I had to do it. If I didn't, I'd die with the rest of them… and I didn't wanna die," he stared across the room at the bare wall as if reading what he had to say.

While he talked, I scanned the room for the phone. My cell

phone was in my purse which was in the principal's office on the other side of the school campus. That now seemed to be at least 500 miles away.

The room was quite dim and seemed too small, too plain to be an office. There was nothing in it but a table with chairs on either side, a small filing cabinet, and a trash can.

On the table sat a desktop computer that was powered off, probably even unplugged, and an arrangement of office supplies normally found on a teacher's desk. What was missing was a telephone.

The scared boy was now silent, so I began to talk, making conversation and asking him questions.

"I'm Lily. What's your name?"

His terrified eyes were wide with worry. "I'm… My name is Des. I'm a freshman."

Freshman. Unbelievable.

"So, is Bryce your friend?"

He shook his head, focusing to his left having just noticed the gun a few yards away. "I never even held a gun before. I didn't know they were so heavy."

Remembering my question, he continued. "Bryce is my older brother. He's 18, a junior, shoulda been a senior and graduating this year. He failed in 8th grade."

I had moved to have my back resting against the wall where the door was. By now an awful deafening emergency siren was going off in the hallway behind my head. Someone pulled the fire alarm. It was so loud the screams and shooting were drowned out.

Realizing he went against his brother's plan, he started banging his head against the wall. "What am I gonna do? He's gonna kill me."

"We need to stay in here until help arrives. And if we're in here, he won't find us, so he can't kill you." I adjusted my position to keep my bruised ankle from being sandwiched underneath me. "So what is all this? What's going on? Tell me Bryce's plan."

With his head still resting on the wall, he looked over at me. "They're planning on killing everyone. The assembly was a perfect time. Everyone's in one spot. You know, required to be there and whatever…"

"Who are *they*?"

"Mostly his friends and others he bullied into joining him—like me." He paused. "They are at every exit. The people leaving would run right into 'em."

Oh, my God. A true massacre.

I closed my eyes and silently prayed for all those kids and teachers. I was sick to my stomach thinking of the families that would get calls of their young children—gone forever or harmed—and having them race to their bedsides. It was impossible to fathom.

"But I couldn't do it. I couldn't hurt anyone. So I found the study lab."

I looked over at him. "What's a study lab?"

"This room. It's a place that students can take tests they've missed or special classes or meetings they have with the counselors or teachers. Whatever," he explained as he used his right forearm to wipe his face.

Study Lab. That made sense. The room was no bigger than an eight-by-eight foot closet. There was a small square window at the top of the door, and high frosted windows on the opposite wall allowed only a small amount of natural light in. I guess it was to keep distractions at a minimum for the student who was to be making up work.

In the seconds I took to think about the room, Des burst into a fit of tears. He kept chanting, *Oh, no! Oh, no!* over and over and rocked back and forth with his head in his hands.

I dug down trying to calm myself enough to speak to him, to use the information I knew to help him. Then I thought about what we needed. "Do you have a phone?"

He looked up at me but didn't take his hands away from his face. His breath caught with tears, and he nodded. Then, with one wet hand, he pulled it from his pocket but before handing it to me he held it in my palm.

"She was s'pose to do somethin'." He whispered.

"I'm sorry. Did you say someone was to do something?" I asked.

He let go of the phone and again wiped his face, this time using his t-shirt. "My aunt. I tried to get her to help."

"How?"

He took a few moments to get his thoughts together before explaining. "I didn't know what to do. When I was in the bathroom getting ready I sent a text to my aunt." He sucked in a deep breath before he continued. "She was the last person I had talked to. I hoped it went through… I guess it… it… I don't think it worked."

With that he hung his head again.

I looked at him and quickly talked as I dialed. "You tried to send for help, to stop this?"

He nodded. "I don't have any friends, the only people besides family in my phone are doing all this—and some of them are family too," he noted, talking about his brother.

"Nine-One-One, what is your emergency?"

The sirens were still blaring in the hall. I had to clasp my hand over my free ear to head the female operator.

"I'm at the school, in Laurel Mountain High School. I'm with a student. We're in a study lab. I don't know if it's safe to come out, but I wanted to tell someone that we're staying in here until told we can leave."

The operator asked a series of questions, took down my information and then asked who was in the hall. "I can't see, there's a small window at the top of the door. I can try." I let her know about my injuries including my ankle.

Hopping up onto one leg I glanced back at Des still curled up in a ball with his back to the wall. Then I looked to the opposite wall where the gun still laid.

The window was too high for me to look out of. "Should I open the door?" I asked. I didn't want to. I wasn't sure of what the situation was like out there.

"No, stay where you are," The operator commanded. "Someone will come to you. Don't open the door until the officers are there."

"Oh my God," I turned around when I heard a thump. Des had pulled the scissors from the pencil holder on the desk and sliced his wrist. He had done it in the matter of seconds it took for me to turn from watching him to trying to look out the window.

"Ma'am?" The operator asked. "Are you still there?"

"Yes! Tell them to hurry, please. I don't know what to do. The boy I'm with, he just cut himself with a scissors. Oh gosh. He's bleeding." I dropped back down to the floor and crawled to his side.

I put the operator on speaker phone and laid the phone down. "Des? Des? Please stay with me." I took off my suit jacket and used the same scissors to cut off the sleeve. I wrapped it around his wrist and pulled tight. As I did so I explained everything to the operator.

I pulled him into my lap and held onto his wrist. I promised to protect him anyway that I could. Watching the blood turn my white camisole a crimson color, I cried. As exhausted and hurt as I was, I didn't fight the tears as they fell. And then I prayed. "Dear Lord, please help us. Protect us from whatever is out there, but we need You just as much in here. Des needs You. Stop the blood—don't let him die. He tried to save everyone. He tried to stop this terrible devastation from happening. Be with us. Be with him."

His eyes were open watching me as I prayed. I looked at him after saying, "Amen," and found him staring at me. I asked him to keep looking at me, to focus on me, and I swore that if he trusted me, I wouldn't leave him.

I realized then that the operator was still on the phone. As I tried to reach it Des began to drift into unconsciousness. I lightly shook him, "No, no, no.... you can't leave. Des? Des?"

As I sat in the corner and pressed the compress to Des' wrist I heard Will in my head. He was talking to a small child, a young boy at the center. Garrett came into the office with his mom. They just left his abusive dad and didn't know where to go. Garrett was crying so hysterically from what he had witnessed at the house that he refused to calm down. After setting Garrett's mom up with a counselor in another room I offered to help with the situation. When I got there Will was asking the small child what his favorite memory was. Was there a place he's been or something that made him happy when he thought about it? Thinking back, I'm not sure what his answer was, but as I closed my eyes, I knew what mine was.

My family was camping in our backyard. We just got a new tent and sleeping bags, and our intentions were to become an adventure-seeking, outdoorsy kind of family. We would spend the whole summer hiking and fishing, and my dad's idea of finding new areas to visit would bring the family together. He was wrong. But before we got to that point, my brother and I were so happy to get to sleep outside under the stars that we began the evening as soon as the last day of school was let out that Friday. We set to building a temporary fire ring to roast marshmallows and fought over who would sleep on which side of the tent. We zipped and unzipped the windows and rearranged sleeping bags until Mom got tired of watching us and made us flip a coin. But the one part that I remember most was the minutes before the sun completely dipped over the horizon. A million lightning bugs floated at the surface of the grass making it appear as if they were rising in waves. It was all around us, and I stood in the middle of the flashing green strobes knowing that this is what heaven would be like.

My eyes flew open to the sounds of heavy footsteps on the floor outside the door. Before I knew what was happening a group of officers burst into the room, handguns raised. I did my best to raise my arms while still holding Des' wrist and keep my mangled jacket wrapped around our arms.

The next five minutes passed in a blur. I remember the young man was carried off to the ambulance. I was helped to my feet and assisted by two officers who acted as crutches on either side of me.

Then, before emerging from the study lab, I did what my body forced me to do at that moment. I close my eyes, refusing to look at the carnage in the hallway.

"*Ms.* Calhoun? Ma'am? Are you still with us?"

I'd gone slack, and they thought I passed out. "I'm okay," I whispered.

"Look at us. Ma'am? Ma'am?" The police officer called for an EMT to bring a gurney.

"I'm okay," I said louder, and this time opened my eyes to look at the officer. What I saw was impossible to believe. I was shocked at what was there.

Nobody. Or perhaps better stated, no bodies.

There were books, papers, and backpacks scattered on the ground. Lockers were open with the contents strewn as far as I could see. But there were no bodies. No blood. I had prepared myself to see the worst. There was nothing. It was almost as if I had a dream. If it wasn't for the siren still piercing the air I would have thought this was just a drill.

Maybe it was.

I was confused, emotionally drained, physically traumatized, and I fought to keep up with officers helping me out the door. As soon as the sun hit me I saw stretchers being loaded into ambulances, awash with every color of emergency light from the multitude of emergency vehicles surrounding the building. I knew then it wasn't a drill.

I was helped into the back of one of those ambulances and one of the officers stayed with me along with an EMT. As the doors shut the officer introduced himself as Detective Michaels. He said he was happy to see me and wanted to ask a few questions. He seemed genuinely kind. I was still in shock, so I nodded slowly in his direction.

He asked for my name and address and why I was at the school that day. I explained I was a speaker at an assembly, but most of what happened was a blur. Then I told him about crawling to the study lab and meeting Des. As we pulled into the medical center, I learned that no one had died, at least as far as Detective Michaels knew. There were only injuries from trying to escape—numerous, but mostly minor.

"How is it possible that nobody died?" I asked

He gave a half smile as if puzzled himself, and said, "Those involved that were outside were caught when warned about what was going to happen through a tip that came in minutes before. I think they said it was a text to an aunt who worked at the police station."

The text from Des.

He saved everyone's lives, and now he was fighting for his.

Chapter 26

I heard the same intercom and beeping. Looking over I expected to see Kory to my left. Instead I was in a single room. My ankle was fractured. My shoulder was just bruised. It hurt worse than the part that was now secured inside a boot. I winced in pain when I attempted to get more comfortable.

From the shadows I heard a familiar voice. "Hey there. You need some more pain meds?"

I puckered up for Will to give me a kiss. After he did I closed my eyes and replied, "You just did."

The nurse walked in, and he told her I was awake and looking like the painkillers had done their job and left. She noted her visit on the board on the wall and then entered something into the computer. Only then did she turn to me and in her best nurse voice ask what my pain was on a 1 to 10 scale.

"I'm okay, really. I don't like to take more medications than I need to. Anyway, I'm wondering about…" I started.

"Now that you're awake, I'll let the doctor on call know. He'll be in shortly," she interrupted.

After she left, I turned to my husband. "Whatever happened with Des?"

He looked at me, confused, before answering. "I'm not sure who Des is. Was he the principal or someone who helped on the scene?"

"Where is the investigator? I vaguely remember speaking with a Mike, Michael something. He was tall, had a bald head."

"Ahh, Detective Michaels. That's who was with you during the ride here in the ambulance. He said he'd be back in the morning to check on you if you were still here or to call him if you went home." He dug a card from his back pocket and handed it to me. "But you need to rest."

"I need to talk to him."

Will just looked at me, but he knew, after this many years of marriage, that the face I gave at that moment would win any battle it was thrown into. So he simply smiled.

I looked up at him and smiled sweetly back at him. "Now tell them to send me home."

Chapter 27

My desk phone rang, and I finished the coffee I was sipping as I picked up.

"Lily, do you have a few minutes?" my assistant Allison was on the phone.

"Sure. What is it?" I replied looking her way. From my office I could see the edge of her cubicle. I could see her tapping a pen as she spoke.

She explained that a Mr. Thompson had stopped by and needed to speak to someone immediately about an emergency. All counselors were on the phone at the moment. I confirmed that Will was busy by the balls rhythmically rising and falling through the glass wall behind me. Looking back in Allison's direction, I saw a middle-aged man by her desk. He had on a gray dress shirt and sweater vest with dark pants. He held something in his hands.

"Have him wait in a meeting room. I'll be right there."

I grabbed my laptop, a notebook, my cell phone, coffee mug, and favorite pen. Through the glass wall I caught Will's eye and used our familiar hand motions to let him know I would be in a meeting and then flashed my phone so he would know to send a text message if something urgent came up.

Sipping my now cooling coffee, I passed Allison who motioned a number three to me as she answered the phone again. Busy day. I smiled and nodded in gratitude.

When I reached the doorway of meeting room three I saw Mr. Thompson was already seated behind the table, and his eyes were downcast staring at the box he had brought with him. "Mr. Thompson?"

He immediately stood and stretched out his right hand. "Call me John."

"Okay John. I'm Lily Calhoun. What brings you in today?" I shut the door behind me and sat in the first chair I came to.

"I'm a guidance counselor at the middle school," John explained.

Hearing that, I was prepared to learn of an event happening at the school or a situation with a student that would require some additional advice on what could be done to solve the problem. What he said next was rather shocking to me.

"Being a counselor for the last 15 years, I've never had such a difficult case. What makes it worse is it involves my own child. My daughter Riley is 16 and is… is pregnant. She got pregnant to keep her boyfriend. Based on what I've found in her room, I don't think it was her idea either." He pushed the box in my direction. "I need to help her but wanted advice from you guys on what to do first."

I opened the lid, and inside were a handful of notes, a dried rose corsage, a set of movie ticket stubs, and a small stuffed animal. Under all of that was a floral, leather-bound book that fit perfectly into the bottom of the box. I assumed it was a journal. I didn't touch anything but knew right away without having to that what he had brought in was a teenage girl's treasure chest, something many girls still had to keep the memories of the boyfriend of the day they claimed as theirs.

"I don't want to open that journal, but I bet you can tell me what it says, can't you?" I asked.

"Well, she's very detailed, that's for sure. But it's concerning that something she's kept from us happened to our little girl and right under own noses."

I looked up at him, and he continued without my encouragement.

"They dated for at least a year that I've known. I thought it was a pretty long time for a high school couple to see each other. He'd come over all the time. They'd watch movies, sometimes we would hang out and all do game night as a family with him there. It was—normal. When she turned 16 I allowed her to finally go out on a date with him, so they'd go bowling, or to the movies… normal dates. A few months ago he stopped coming by. Riley said they were still together. I guess I didn't think anything of it, but then one day she came home in tears. She admitted to her mom that they slept together and that she thought she was pregnant."

He swallowed loudly and I knew the worst part was to come.

"If you read the journal, you'd see that there was something else that was going on. Sam, that's Riley's boyfriend, well he had another girlfriend—Brandi. And that Brandi girl was threatening to harm Riley. I know because I read it, in there." He pointed to the box.

"So do you think she got pregnant on purpose?" I asked.

"I know she did." Again he nodded toward where the answers were, in the journal.

"Teenagers, especially girls, can be so cruel. Boys tend to be brought up to defend themselves, to brush off bad words, bullies, and heartbreak. Girls aren't as lucky. It sometimes sneaks up on them and can have the most harmful, lasting, and sadly… sadly devastating results." I frowned.

"Sounds personal? You don't seem to be old enough to have teenagers," he noted.

I huffed out a small laugh. "No teenagers yet, but between working here and what happened to me growing up during my teenage years I have plenty of resources to reference."

I could see the defeat in John's eyes. His resources were that he was a guidance counselor, and they weren't enough in this situation. He was not only failing at what his job should, but also with his daughter and family. "I should have seen the signs. I should have known something like this was happening. I'm… I've been blindsided."

"Parents usually are." And then I began to tell him how I chose my career path.

I wasn't afraid to expose what happened to me. I told the story often. It was still painful for me to hear, myself. But in a way it was reassurance of survival. I felt stronger, almost as if I climbed up another rung on a ladder each time I relived the moments of my hospital stay. The look on each person's face that hears it varies from pity to pain. I try not to let them feel sorry for me, never staying too long on the depression and recovery part.

Holly's story, to me, is more important than even my own. She led me through the worst times and introduced me to my best times. I like to use her story and how she helped me as an example with clients. I also told John Des' story. His is fresh and more relevant to people when talking about teenage issues. Many people still remember the news coverage from that day, although that was three months ago. Both people crossed my path for the exact reason—I needed them. Even though each was a hard situation for me to endure at the time, I was changed for the better because of Holly and Des.

"Wow. I guess no matter what she'll always be my little Riley."

"I think you're still in shock. This is too fresh for you. Sadly, most of the time it's also when people make the worst decisions. I want to give you something, John."

From my portfolio notebook, I took my business card and tore off a sheet of blank, lined paper. I handed him the card and then started to write websites and phone numbers of some of the other people and literature that would help through the tough times they were all facing as a family.

"If you, or your wife, or even Riley need anything, please do not hesitate to call me, okay?" I was sincere in my words and honest with my help.

Chapter 28

*T*he gala I was in charge of organizing was being held to raise money for our non-profit business. My job as marketing director was the most important in the planning process. I was making arrangements for the conference center, designing the flyers, and promoting the event. The price of the ticket included dinner and entertainment. We were also hosting a silent auction throughout the entire night. Will had left the office three hours before me to get Emmy from the daycare before they closed.

There was so much to do, and as I finished one task I thought of something else to make the event even more special. I was having fun. I enjoyed finding people to volunteer services or donate goods. I loved thinking of people to invite and how decorations and seating needed to be arranged to get the most people into the venue. Seating charts, auction bid sheets, and menus needed to be created. What could be delegated was, but I kept some of the best parts of what the evening would hold to myself. This is what I was made to do.

I was finally leaving the office at 7:30 when a picture from my bookshelf caught my eye. It had been sitting there since I moved into the office and in fact traveled with me to every desk I moved to; from my bedroom, to my dorm room, to every place in this office complex. It was a framed snapshot of Kory and me. We were both leaving the room that day, and we promised to keep in touch. She would be checking out of the hospital and going home. I was being moved to two floors up for psychiatric assessment and recurrent monitoring. It sounded painful. It wasn't. But it *was* embarrassing, especially having to tell a girl that instead of leaving the hospital they were testing me for craziness.

I hugged Kory's frail body. She whispered in my ear, "I'm praying for you. I know you'll get better. Just take care of yourself and know there are angels watching over you always."

She was an angel. Hearing her sweet words made my move to the new floor a little easier. She even came to visit me during my stay there. She had a follow up appointment at her pulmonologist, and I was a pit stop for her. Every year we exchanged birthday gifts and Christmas cards. For several years it was something I unconsciously looked forward to. Kory passed away during her junior year. She was 17—the same age I was when I tried to end my life. That was over 11 years ago, but I remember that funeral like it was yesterday. It was the hardest thing I ever had to experience.

Kory was still on my mind when I walked through the front door. Emmy was playing in the living room with her favorite baby doll. She was winding the doll's big blond curls around and clipping the loops down to her head with big barrettes. "Mommy! Look—I braided hers hair."

She was so sweet. "She's beautiful. Just like you." I kissed the top of her head and then walked into Will's awaiting arms. "It was I long day," I told him.

"The gala will be so successful. It'll be worth it"

I sighed into his shoulder. "I sure hope so."

The house smelled of spaghetti, so I followed my nose to the kitchen. "Dinner looks good. I'm starving."

He followed me to the stove and lightly caressed my back as he reached into the refrigerator and pulled out a bottle of wine. He knew it was a day for one of my rare glasses of wine. As he poured, I dished out noodles. "How was Emmy's evening?"

"Oh, she's fine. Dinner was actually her idea. She told me she wanted 'sketti or poptarts. Even though poptarts were easier, I thought health-wise spaghetti was the better choice.

I laughed and slurped down a noodle. Hearing her name Emmy

came into the kitchen and was now holding onto my leg. I ran my fingers through her curls, and she sat on my foot for a free ride to the table. While I ate she and her dolly shared space under table. Will washed the dishes and told a story of Emmy dancing to a toddler show on cable. We laughed as she demonstrated again, and I fell even deeper in love with my life.

One thing I don't remember doing when I awoke in the hospital after my suicide attempt was thanking God for saving me and keeping me on earth to live my life longer. I guess it was because my dreams of my future were dim or even forgotten to me at that time. But now, laying in this bed, here in my house, I didn't let another moment pass before I folded my hands, closed my eyes, and told Him of my appreciation for saving me once again.

Funny how my life's rollercoaster pulled back into the station just at the right moment to show a person that she could survive anything it could throw at her.

Chapter 29

*M*en are lucky. Their dress wardrobe requires one nice suit, of any color, really. Will is double lucky in that he has two in his closet—a gray one and black one. Along with that, he owns two ties, a black vest, and a few dress shirts in a variety of neutrals and pastels. He literally is set for a good 25 or 30 engagements based on the different combinations he could create with those articles of clothing.

I, on the other hand, have two formal gowns from when I was a bridesmaid in a couple weddings. Both are completely outdated and out of style. I also own a few strappy sundresses. They are *not* formal attire.

So here I am—less than eight hours before the gala that I organized with nothing to wear. Will has 28 choices. I didn't even have a budget to buy a dress.

"I'm taking Emmy to Thrift Alley. We're having a girls' day together before I take her to Dad's house for the evening."

Will poked his head around the hall corner as he walked by. "Okay—I think."

Thrift Alley isn't an actual name of a store. It was, in fact, a block of stores—consignment, vintage, and secondhand—that was popular among young adults and the elderly. My age range wasn't in the target customer range. Knowing this, I assumed I'd still be able to hide my *mom-bod* among the racks and weave my way around displays of abandoned prom dresses hoping a cheap-priced one would just magically appear in my cart. With the many stores and choices, there had to be something I could use for the event.

"Wait, have you still not picked up a dress for tonight?"

I shook my head. "I'm not worried about it. I'll find some-thing. Worst case, I've made do before with a lot less to work with. Remember Katelynn's *beached* wedding?"

By the *beached* wedding, I referred to the hurricane that canceled a good friend's wedding shortly after Will and I were married. Not only did we have to immediately evacuate the oceanfront resort area, we ended up with one less suitcase in the shuffle—the one with our wedding outfits.

The downsized ceremony was moved inland to a small chapel that could accommodate the remaining guests who stayed, us included. With only a day's notice I was able to put together dress clothes comprised of items from a gas station, a dollar bargain outlet, and even Benny's Hardware & Plumbing—the only three stores in that small community.

Knowing I was more than capable, Will bid us good-bye on our way out the door and promised I'd come home to a freshly mowed yard.

Chapter 30

*T*he first store I went into was Metro Retro. The dance music blared as I opened the door. It was a mix between disco and techno. Every head turned when Emmy and I walked in, and all conversation was dropped. It was awkward to say the least. I was out of place. They knew it—and it didn't take long for me to figure that out either. I even found myself oddly apologizing as I exited after a quick loop around the store.

"Let's not do that again," I told Emmy as we headed toward the next store, appropriately named, Next to New.

No music greeted me, nor did surprised and irritated faces. Instead, the distinct smell of a grandma's attic met me at the entrance. The bell indicated my arrival, and a voice answered from the backroom, "I'll be out in two seconds."

I quickly looked around. Emmy spotted a pile of high heels in the corner and took off in that direction to play dress-up. I started browsing the racks of dresses along the side wall. I wasn't more than a few dresses into the display when my mouth physically dropped open. There was a black chiffon strapless gown with a rhinestone beaded bodice. It looked like was something straight out of the Academy Awards. Remarkably, it was also my size.

"That one is beautiful, isn't it?" A voice startled me from behind.

I turned and looked into the smiling face of a short middle-aged woman. A crown of blonde ringlets framed a face which held bifocals on the end of her nose. A sparkly chain draped across her neck to keep her from losing them. Behind her ear, practically lost in her sprout of hair, was a #2 pencil. She reminded me of a home economics teacher.

"It is. In fact, it's the most gorgeous gown I've ever seen—or touched." I ran the soft fabric through my fingers.

"Rumor has it Miss North Carolina wore it."

My eyes widened. "Really?"

"No, dear, I have no idea. Makes for a good story though, huh?" The lady laughed deeply before introducing herself. "I'm Rosie, and this is my little shop. I'll let you browse around. Let me know if you need anything."

Chapter 31

I didn't need to browse long. I bought that dress—and not because it might have been worn by Miss North Carolina. Okay, maybe somewhere in the back of my mind that's why I got it, but it was more because of the hospitality of the salesperson, and the way it fit me like a glove, and the price. When I stepped out from behind the changing room curtain Emmy clapped her hands and called me a princess. Rosie gasped and covered her mouth while shaking her head back and forth, her glasses going along for the ride.

I had black strappy satin heels at home, but Rosie encouraged me to buy matching rhinestone broaches to embellish the fronts of them. For under six dollars, it would be like I bought a new pair just for the occasion. I also found a bracelet and single rhinestone pendant to top off the ensemble, and I was able to get it all at this one store. Rosie hugged me as I left. As I turned to thank her she disappeared, I supposed back to the storage room from which she first emerged. Or maybe, like Cinderella, she was my fairy god-mother and just appeared to help me for my ball only to evaporate into thin air once I was all set.

Emmy squeezed my hand. "Mommy, since you're a princess, can we do your hair now?"

I hadn't thought about what to do with the rest of me. I knew how to create a hairdo and put on *night out* makeup, but I also knew my limits, and a formal event like the gala was certainly well outside those lines. "I guess we can. But only if you get your hair done too."

A big smile flew across Emmy's cheeks, and she began to bouncing excitedly. "Okay. Yes, yes, yes."

The last thing I wanted to do was spend a little on a dress and then a ton on a hair style. Emmy and I sat on a bench eating hotdogs from a sidewalk vendor's cart. I thought about my options, which were few. I usually got my haircut at the place with the best coupon. I didn't really consider myself ever having a stylist. Then, as if needing to talk to my fairy godmother again, Rosie, the home-ec teacher lookalike, came walking down the sidewalk at that moment. She didn't notice me as she crossed to get a hotdog as well, but I waved in her direction as she took the foil wrapped lunch from the cashier.

"Fancy seeing you again." She walked in my direction.

"You as well." I patted the seat beside me for her to join us.

"No, I can't—nobody runs that shop but me, so I must get back. But where are you off to next?" she asked.

As I wiped Emmy's face free of dripping ketchup, she talked through the napkin, "Mommy's getting her hair done like a real princess."

"Is she?"

I giggled. "Yeah, just trying to think of where a good, not overly pricey stylist is around here."

"That would be "Barb's Bobs and Bows."

"Like Cinderella!" Emmy shouted. "Bibby bibb…bibbey bobby boo!"

I looked at her. "Something like that." Then I turned to Rosie. "Where is this place?"

"Well Barb is my neighbor, and I've known her forever. Her shop is about two blocks around the corner there." She motioned with her hotdog-free hand. "She's very reasonable and even more talented. You'll be in good hands with her. Miss North Carolina has nothing on you as you are right now, But just wait until she works her magic wand on you."

I nodded once. "Well, Rosie, I must say, you really are my fairy godmother aren't you?"

I don't know what kind of fairy dust or magic powers Rosie used, but we were able to get into Barb's salon ten minutes later. A coloring appointment canceled, and ironically she didn't have anyone else on standby to take the spot. She curled my hair, painted my face, and even gave Emmy a cute French twist with curls. In just over an hour we were spun around in our chairs to face the mirrors of change. I was floored. I looked exactly like a princess from a child's movie, and if I was the dirty, poor, underwhelming girl when I walked in—I was the beautiful and regaled woman that Prince Charming fell head over heels for when I walked out.

Oh boy! Will was in trouble.

Chapter 32

We arrived at the gala in style. Will rented a town car to drop us off at the red-carpeted entry.

"Promise me that was the only time riding in the town car tonight? I can't imagine how much it cost you for the 15-minute drive to get here," I whispered into his ear after taking his extended arm.

He leaned in close to kiss my cheek, then whispered back, "I promise. No more town car, but you needed to arrive in something as beautiful as you are tonight."

I smiled and blushed. After all this time together, he still made me so happy.

The gala was being held in a private wing of the city museum. The space was donated for the evening by the curator Louis Ernst, with only one request—raise a lot of money for the organization. Louis was a close friend of Will's father. His family spent a lot of time at events at the museum, and eventually the friendship grew outside the walls of exhibits. Will called him Uncle Lou, and it was wonderful for him to allow us to invade his place for the evening. It was Uncle Lou that I saw first as we made our way inside. I hugged him tightly and thanked him again for everything.

"It's so perfect. You did an amazing job setting everything up," he replied back as I pulled away.

Two ushers stood on either side of the entrance. Knowing who we were, they only nodded in our direction instead of asking to escort us inside.

As soon as the space opened up to the lobby I saw what Lou was talking about. Some guests had already arrived and were milling around the entryway which was lined with children's art that was placed on display for bidding.

All pieces were made and donated by students of the city's art enrichment program. Everything from painted portraits and landscapes to pottery and abstract art were up for auction.

To the left was an arrangement of tables holding over 200 entries to a silent auction that would continue throughout the evening. Some items for bid had people standing four people deep to add their offers to the list. All of the participation made me excited for how the evening might go.

"Mr. and Mrs. Calhoun." A server pushed a tray of champagne toward us, and we each took a flute.

"I feel famous," I said, still holding on to Will's arm.

"You kind of are," he replied out of the corner of his mouth.

The lobby was pumping with excitement, but the dining hall at the opposite side of the venue exuded calmness. It was subdued in nature; relaxed and tranquil.

The musical entertainment for the cocktail and dinner hours would be by City-side Musicians, a non-profit inner-city group of jazz musicians. They were already set up and playing. There were only a few people at the tables, but those in the room were in hushed conversation. When they saw us enter they all stood.

"See," Will whispered.

I only smiled in returned and then walked toward the guests, thanking them with handshakes. They replied with *congratulations* and *good work on the lovely evening.*

It *was* a lovely evening, but I knew it could only get better from that moment.

Chapter 33

*T*he museum room that we used held 24 round tables. The ones closest to the makeshift stage were reserved for the higher-donation-per-plate guests, but I was told the special guest speaker would be worth it. I hoped that was true. This was the one part of the evening I wasn't involved with and didn't have any prior knowledge of. Will told me he would take care of it and to trust him. So I did. I was just anxious to find out who it would be.

The decorations I decided on were contemporary but with classic undertones. Dim lighting with featured spotlights shed columns of light along the burgundy-draped walls. There was a theater feel to it. A handful of arrangements donated from a local florist sat on tall pedestals around the room. Candelabras allowed for subtle lighting without the harsh fluorescents turned on overhead. It was perfect.

As the evening continued the dining hall began to fill with the guests who already bid on items in the lobby. Men with naturally frosted hair and full pockets were evenly spaced around rented tables topped with donated linens, homemade centerpieces, and borrowed china. Their wives sipped coffee and wine, both out of cups that would be reused for a wedding the following week. I laughed knowing that the budget was nonexistent, yet the ambiance and décor was exquisite. It would be my secret to keep.

Chapter 34

*A*s the jazz band played on, dinner was served among the clinking of glassware. A buzz of conversation over plates ensued, and laughter mixed with stories of careers and families among the members of each table.

The volunteer servers removed plates, replacing dinner remnants with double-crusted pies and seven-layered cakes and flavored coffees. Will and I mingled, making sure to shake every hand or hug those guests we were close with. As the last desserts were passed out, Will made his way to the stage, and the background music faded. A small podium sat stage right, and he adjusted the microphone before speaking.

"Welcome guests—or should I say *friends*. I want to thank every single one of you for coming. If I haven't already shaken your hand, don't worry. You aren't forgotten. I will before the night is over."

Light laughter waved across the dining hall.

Will continued, "Our keynote speaker tonight is someone you may have heard of, especially you sports fans out there. As first round draft pick in the NFL last year, he became one of the youngest players to join the football league. His ability on the field has earned him an amazing career future. He is more than a name on a football jersey seen Sunday afternoons on television screens. He is our good friend. I am honored to know him for who he is and what he represents. And I want all of you to have that same privilege. So with that, please join me in welcoming Charlie Frizell."

Audience applause accompanied Will's hug with the towering man who joined him at the podium. Silent smiles were exchanged, and Will patted Charlie's back as thanks and encouragement for him volunteering his time and story.

Charlie readjusted the mic to fit his larger statue and began his story. He was a product of long-term foster care. It started when he was four years old, and his dad was arrested. His mom abandoned him less than two years later and he was left in his great-grandpa's care. When the old man was transferred to a nursing home, Charlie was placed in foster care.

He would spend the next ten years of his young life being shuffled from house to house, foster family to foster family. Then, at the age of 16, his path went from bad to worse. The family he was with moved to the country to keep him from the gang life he was becoming involved with. He had stolen for initiation, and on the night of the theft he witnessed his friend get shot by a rival gang. They dropped his body off at the emergency room and left to avoid being implicated in either the theft or the shooting. His friend later died.

But Charlie was no country boy, and felt he couldn't live outside of the city. He rebelled against his foster parents and eventually ran away, stealing their car and his foster mom's credit card. He ended up in a group home. Within six months he not only failed school but ended up in juvenile detention. It was there that he was introduced to the Hope and Wellness Organization.

While in the detention center, Charlie put his full attention into learning. He wanted to go to college one day, though he felt he had blown any chance he might have had. One day Will visited the detention center to talk with the kids. Charlie was in the room that day, and that chance encounter was when he got his second chance at life.

He finished with this statement, "I was almost 17 when I found my permanent home. I can honestly say I never would have done it without Will and Lily and everyone at Hope and Wellness. I know that sounds cliché, but that's okay. I'm okay with the way it it sounds because it's true. There's no other way to put it. I am who I am because of them. They do so much good for people who feel they don't deserve it. How many other places open their doors and their hearts to the messiest misfits and never think twice about it. Thank you guys. For my life."

The round of applause grew, and people stood one by one around the room. Women wiped tears as the men allowed pride to show on their face. Some of them also had glossy eyes.

Will hugged Charlie longer this time and more silent exchange was given between the two men. A chuckle from both sealed the conversation, and Will once again stepped up to the podium.

"I want to tell one more story about my friend Charlie," he said as the room hushed and people returned to their seats. "One of the first conversations I had with him came from a request he had when we first talked. Charlie asked me for a Bible. A simple request. He said they had an old one at the detention center, but when he left he couldn't take it. Even if he wanted to it wouldn't be fair to anyone else wanting to learn about God. I told him by the end of the day I'd make sure he got one. There was a used book store a few blocks away, and I went in with one purpose. I was getting a Bible that day for Charlie. There were three on the shelf, and I picked the one with the best cover. Even with the inscription to someone named Fran in the front cover it was perfect. I scrawled under Fran's name *and then to Charlie—keep this Bible moving to the next person.*"

Will paused and looked around the room before continuing, "I want to let everyone know that it was Charlie that made me order the cases of Bibles that line our walls at the center, from children's to the King James, to large print, and the Bible on disk. Anyone who wants one—gets one. And it's because of him.

"So thank you Charlie—for what you've done for our lives."

After Charlie spoke there was an hour of musical entertainment by Heidi Sinclair, an up and coming adult contemporary artist. Will did very well with his selections for special guest and entertainment, and everyone, including me, was amazed at how such a big name in talent was in the room with them at that moment.

Will explained that Heidi was born to a young mother in foster care. It would take almost two years for her to be adopted by her parents, and she was now an advocate helping other adoptive parents through the long process. She had called a few months before to donate some money and supplies to a food drive we were hosting. She said anytime we needed her she'd be there. And here she was. Will even kept it a surprise from me.

That man. He was my rock star.

Between songs, Allison, my assistant, announced final bids would be accepted for the next ten minutes.

"Sounds like time for a much needed break," Heidi added. "Plus, I can't miss out on the special package I have my eye on."

Everyone laughed, and a surge of people filled the lobby. People volleyed for the win as they went back and forth with pens like a tennis match.

Finally, after what felt like hours, Allison called "Pens down!"

Everyone stepped back from the tables in unison, and I breathed a sigh of relief. That was tense.

While totals from the silent auction and art sale were tallied and added to the dinner donations, our musical guest once again took to the stage.

I pulled up a chair with Allison in the lobby to help count bids. "Yes! I got it!" She said holding a paper to her chest.

"What did you get?"

"The package I was bidding on. I practically had to stand guard to make sure I got it. And *ha*—I did."

I would have asked more about her prize, but I was in utter shock at what I saw before me. Gift cards were going at triple face value. Haircuts for $200. Artwork was coming off the walls no less than $500 each.

People were overly generous, and my $50,000 goal was more than tripling before my eyes. As money was counted and totals were updated, I was speechless. During my closing remarks, tears accompanied every word, and I was forced to close my eyes to focus on what I needed to say.

Afterward people swarmed the stage to give us hugs and promises to be there to support us every year we held the event. That night, with that one event, the center raised over $180,000.

Chapter 36

We were still giving hugs and thanking our guests when Will took my arm. Then he looked at those guests closed to us and apologized. "I hate to drag her away, but it's important that I take Lily with me at this time."

Everyone nodded approval and resumed talking to one another. Will ushered me toward the front door. "Where are we going? We can't leave." I stopped just shy of the exit.

"But we have to. Our chariot awaits. And we can't let it turn back into a pumpkin." Will opened the door.

There at the bottom of the steps a driver held the back door of a limo open, inviting us in. I looked at Will who only smiled. I looked back to the limo, and the driver beckoned to the open door with his right hand and a nod.

"You only said no more town cars. *This*—is a limo," Will explained before I said anything.

I put my clutch under my arm and let him lead me to the waiting car. Before getting in, I turned to Will and asked, "Let me guess, it's not taking us home, is it?"

Will shook his head and simply smiled. In his hands he held up the bid sheet Allison had to guarded so carefully. It was a certificate to a bed & breakfast outside of town.

That man.

Chapter 37

"Someday I want a horse."

We had been lying in bed, in the dark. I'd been staring at the ceiling for the past 20 minutes, and based on Will's breathing I knew he wasn't asleep either.

"You do?"

"I always have. Doesn't every little girl dream of having a horse? Asking for one for Christmas?"

"I don't know. I've never been a little girl." He laughed.

"Well they do. And Emmy will one day say she wants one too."

"So one day we'll get a horse."

I paused, sighing before continuing. "But we live in a subdivision. I doubt the homeowners association will allow it."

"True. I guess we need to start looking for a house in the country."

"Wow. That conversation went far fast."

"Okay, let's just decide whether we want French toast or waffles for breakfast first."

"Good idea." I kissed his forehead and closed my eyes. "Waffles." I said after a few seconds of silence.

"Plain of blueberry?"

"Hmmm… too many decisions." I turned over.

"How about this. I'll see what they are serving in the morning, and then I'll surprise just you," Will whispered, and I drifted off to sleep.

Chapter 38

*A*s my Wednesday morning after the Gala began, the excitement of the fundraiser was dying down. I had just sat down at my desk with my coffee when something Charlie had said that night came back to me. *There is never a time that is too late. The right people are everywhere they just need to be found.*

My desk was bare, yet I felt that there was more to be done. I thought about an adoption that a desperate mom needed for her children and the other party that longed for the children they couldn't have. Both came through the office, but once they get their connections that I put them in touch with, I no longer see the outcome. In the past files were placed in the cabinet with a quick checkmark of completion. I needed to change that. From now on I'd take the extra time to ensure the right process was done for the person, not the paperwork.

I remembered from the other night how Charlie talked about how he was told by a caseworker that his eyes didn't shine like they should. They had a sadness in them. I remembered it with Garrett years ago when he was in the office. That same sadness was in Des's eyes in the school that fateful day. He needed help and didn't get it until it was too late.

Maybe it wasn't too late—even now.

I picked up the phone and dialed.

"Allison. Can you help me find someone?"

If nothing else, I needed to find out if the young man was okay and was getting the help he needed.

Chapter 39

*I*t's the last weekend in June. The ocean breeze feels wonderful this evening as I sit here on the terrace of Donatella's Café. My head is pounding though. I know stress is to blame.

Tomorrow is Brandon's wedding. Part of me still can't believe we got an invitation. As I sit at the table at the rehearsal dinner with my family and look at the couple, I don't even recognize the guy. He's grown up. He seems happy. He's got a great job and a nice house. But I truly don't know him. We haven't said more than perfunctory *hello* and *how are you* in so many years that I don't know if I remember his voice.

Mom isn't here yet. She is flying in later tonight. She is an RN now. She works in the pediatric wing of the hospital helping kids, even troubled ones like I was. Maybe my suicide attempt is what led her down that road. I don't know, and I doubt she'll ever tell me.

Her shift ends at 7:00 and then she's driving straight to the airport and should arrive on the 10:35 flight from Knoxville. I'm nervous to see her, to spend time with her. But I feel like it's time. It's much needed for me, and I know that she's probably just as nervous as I am. We've talked over the years—even seen each other on occasion—but this is the first time we will all be around each other as a family since Brandon moved out for college.

Will will take the kids back to the hotel after dinner, and then I'll pick Mom up at the airport. I told her I would, even though I just wanted to crawl into bed and shove a pillow over my head in hopes of suffocating the pain. I down four pain killers with my champagne as the couple is toasted by Brandon's best man.

My aunt and uncle sit to my right. Gina was married to my

dad's brother, Tim. He was a mail carrier, and she was a substitute teacher at the high school. She loved her job but wanted the flexibility to do things and go places when she wanted, so she never committed to a full-time position even though the school system desperately needed teachers. They also didn't have children. It said a lot about who she was as a person. Tim was oblivious and just enjoyed her company.

To our left is a couple that Brandon graduated with from high school. I knew them well and found myself drawn to talking to them most of the night while Dad and Tim chatted on the other side of me.

"I'm surprised you aren't in the wedding," I told Dawson.

"Yeah, well I'm not. Brandon withdrew from us when he moved over here."

"And you, sister of the groom, aren't even in the wedding," Brianna noted.

"I don't really know Cassidy that well. You'd think after almost a decade she'd be the sister I never had."

Brianna paused. "They seem happy though."

"They do, don't they? That's why I'm shocked they haven't visited more."

As the dinner winds down, Will kisses my cheek and tells me to be careful on my trip to the airport and that he'll see me later. I give Emmy a big hug and eskimo kisses before turning back to my husband. "I love you."

"More than you know," he answers.

As I sit sideways in the chair watching Emmy shuffle behind, Will waves to me as she walked backwards. I blow her a kiss, and am surprised when a hand touched my shoulder. I'm even more surprised when I turned around, and instead of seeing Dad, Brandon was standing beside me.

"Can we talk?"

Chapter 40

*T*he guests had gone home or back to their hotel rooms. Cassidy left with her parents. She was traditional in that she wouldn't see Brandon again until the next day when she walked down the aisle. I still had an hour and a half before Mom's flight came in, so I agreed to have a drink with Brandon at the bar.

Even though I should have ordered a glass of red wine to compliment the fancy dress I wore, I stuck with a Shirley temple instead knowing I'd be driving soon. I didn't want to take the chance, especially in an area I was unfamiliar with. Since I rarely drank I only had the one toasting glass of champagne two hours before. That was plenty for me for the night.

Brandon followed my lead and ordered a plain cola. I respected that choice. It wasn't much, something he didn't even need to do, but it was nice to see him make choices a gentleman would make. It made me smile.

After receiving our drinks, I offered him my congratulations. I was happy he was finally making the commitment.

"That's an odd thing to say." He laughed.

"I just mean that you've been with her for so long that Cassidy's already practically family."

He looked at me. "Are you sure you feel that way?"

"Brandon if you're happy, and she makes you a better person, then I'm excited for you."

"You didn't even get close to answering my question."

I looked back at him and ran my tongue over my teeth thinking about my next words carefully. "Okay. Truth?"

He just nodded.

"I don't know her. I've never had the chance to get to know her. I'd like to. She might be the sister I never had. She might be best-friend material. That's something I haven't had in a long time. But I don't know her. All I know is that the longer you've been with her the further you've been from us."

"Ouch," he acted hurt. "You think she's the reason I don't come around?"

"Brandon, don't you think we'd like to see you more often? Your family is on the other side of the state, but you're here making a new life with new family."

He took a long drink and left the straw between his lips a few seconds longer. "I'm sorry you don't know her, because you're wrong about Cassidy."

"Maybe I am. I don't know. But I know you. Or at least I did. I'm sorry I messed up. I'm sorry my actions and decisions made you leave. I hurt a lot—"

He stopped me and reached for my hand. "Lily. I *never* left because of you. I wanted to help you. I tried to help you. I even talked to Mom and Dad about quitting soccer so we could all be together and make it all better."

I stared at him, confused. "When? I don't remember any of that."

"I came to visit you in the hospital."

I remembered the one day he visited when I was on the pediatric wing, before my stay in Crazy Town. He didn't stay long. He seemed mad that day. He never came back after that.

"I told Mom I wasn't going to the tournament that next weekend. I was staying home, and I thought we should all do the same."

I nodded. "Yeah, she talked about you having to go out of town. She mentioned you might go on your own but that she would stay with me. By the next weekend I was already moved to the *other* floor. I couldn't have visitors, and I just told her to go too."

He agreed, pain entering words as he thought about the psychiatric testing and observation. "Right, I remember. That's not what we talked about at home though."

He explained that he refused to go to the tournament, even after I was moved to the *other* floor. He told Mom that family was more important than a sport. She got angry at him and told him he would end his college career by talking like that. He was adamant about not playing. Dad is the one that stepped in and convinced him to go. He was mad that day because of them. Not her.

I hung my head as I listened to his story. Closing my eyes, I tried to keep the tears at bay. I was hurt. I was sad. I was still confused, but what Brandon had yet to say was the part of his story that literary broke my heart.

Chapter 41

$\mathcal{B}$y now I was turned sideways on my stool, and my drink was mostly forgotten about. I had wiped my eyes with the napkin my drink was supposed to sit on.

"I'm sorry Lily. I didn't mean to make you sad."

"I've just lived with guilt for so long. I didn't know there was more to the story. It's hard to hear that when you're so convinced otherwise. I … I can't explain it."

"I know. You don't have to."

I pushed loose hairs behind my ear and ran my fingers to the ends of my hair. It was a habit I had when I was nervous. "So you played in that tournament, right?"

He nodded. "I did. And we won." Then he switched gears. "I prayed for you. I wanted you to get better, and I was sad that whatever happened to you before made you think that you had to do—that."

I knew he didn't know everything. While we were confessing secrets I told him the entire story from Whitney and her jealous actions to Ty and what he did in the stairwell.

A furious look came over Brandon's face. "Why didn't you tell me? I never liked him. He would have had to face me had I known."

"I didn't want you to get hurt too. By the time it all fell apart I wasn't looking for help." I paused. "I just wanted it done."

This time Brandon leaned in and hugged me. "I should have done this years ago."

"Thank you," I whispered, and this time the tears fell fast and freely.

He pulled away and handed me his drink napkin, and I asked him the question that brought us to that bar in the first place.

"So why did you leave, and why haven't you come back around?"

"I guess because I'm as guilty as you when it came to wanting to run away."

I gave a sarcastic snort. "Run away?"

"Yeah. I was mad at Mom and Dad. I couldn't face them—especially losing one of my best friends. It really only got worse after that weekend."

I looked at Brandon and he shifted on his stool. Calling the bartender over, I pointed at our glasses. I could tell me were going to need refills for this.

Chapter 42

"*Y*ou caught them?"

"Yes. I. Did." Brandon nodded with each word.

"How? Where?" I really didn't want to know the answers but I had to.

"We had a tournament tradition. We'd order pizzas and the entire group would meet and eat together in a lobby or outside somewhere at the hotel where we stayed. We were all sitting outside by the pool, and the pizzas had just arrived, and I couldn't find Mom. I went upstairs and just as the elevators opened I could hear a woman's voice coming from Franklin's room. He just happened to have the room directly in front of the elevator.

"Anyway, he didn't bring his wife along, so I was intrigued. Nosy, I guess, was more like it. After a few seconds I turned to go back down and get Alec, but just as I did so the door opened, and Franklin came out buttoning his shirt. Behind him, Mom stood in nothing but a bed sheet. A bed sheet! Can you imagine?"

My eyes told him the answer. They were as wide as saucers.

He continued, "I was irate. I was devastated. I was shocked. I was so many things at that moment that I couldn't move."

"Did she see you?"

"Of course. And she tried to apologize for the rest of the trip. Do you know what the hardest part to swallow was?"

I shook my head.

"Alec knew."

"What?!"

"Yup. After getting out of there I ran to find him. When I told him he wasn't surprised. He said he thought I knew and that he thought it was over, that his dad had told him months ago that it was."

"Months ago? How long was it going on?"

He took a deep breath. "At least two years."

I gasped. "Oh my God."

"I know, right? I couldn't talk to Alec anymore. We were so close, but he kept that from me. I couldn't handle it. Friends just don't do that to each other."

I thought about our father. "Did Dad know?"

Shaking his head he answered, "I never told him. But he had to know. He just gave up on their marriage. It was like he was deflated, that he didn't even want to try. It just made me so freaking mad. I never wanted to be the kid from a broken family, and ours was as broken as they came."

Chapter 43

My eyes shot up from the bar as I came to a realization. She moved because she ran away too.

"Franklin wasn't gonna leave his wife for Mom, and she couldn't go home. She couldn't face Dad again, not after two years or more of lying. And how do you think she felt about what she did to us?"

"Wow, that's—it's all so much to take in. I feel like I've been watching a movie for years only to come to the end where the entire thing was a major twist, something the writers add to make you question your entire movie experience."

"I know, Sis." He breathed a big sigh as if getting this off his chest was his last mission in life.

Anger I felt toward Mom was now laced with a new feeling—sadness. I was sad that she felt the need to leave her family for her indiscretions. First me, then Mom, and Brandon—Dad was the only one who didn't run away. I guess he handled his feelings better than us, or maybe he didn't deal with them at all.

From the clock behind the bar I saw that it was 9:57, time to head west toward the airport. Even though it was only ten minutes away I wanted to be early, to greet Mom by baggage claim. It was more personal than waiting in the cell phone parking area and driving up to whisk someone from the curbside before the airport security ushered you out of the pick-up lane.

To my left Brandon continued to air his concerns, a welcome sound. "You hear about parents that stay together until their kids are out of school and then divorce. They stay together *for the kids* but in the end the kids, whether grown are not, get hurt, sometimes wishing the problem could have been addressed years ago, just get it over with. Makes me think we were blind to being that kind of family."

"Yeah at least those families know what's going on."

"Exactly."

"To be honest, I'm okay now. It's taken me a while, and the distance helped, but I'm better. Dad and Maggie are doing okay, right?"

"Yeah, they are. She's a great woman for him. Just what he needs."

He continued. "I don't know if Mom found what she's looking for, but I hope she's happy."

Something told me she was the only one *not* doing well. I needed to see her. Although I was scared to have to face reality, I had to find out for myself.

"It's almost ten o'clock. I need to start heading toward the airport. I really enjoyed… well, really *needed* this. Thank you."

He got up from his stool first. "If it's okay I'd really like to ride with you. I have nothing else to do tonight, and I doubt I'll be sleeping too much, especially having to be all by myself."

I grinned, glad he was going to be with me. "I'd like that. Mom will certainly be surprised."

I took my seat behind the wheel, and as Brandon got into the passenger seat, he pulled a small envelope from his back pocket and handed it to me across the middle console. My name was scrawled in airy cursive across the front.

"It's from Cassidy. I don't know what it says, but she wanted me to give it to you."

"Really? Hmm. Well, thank you—or thank her for me." I deposited it in my purse and started the car.

Chapter 44

*W*e had a little under 20 minutes before the plane was set to land. The airport had a nice, glassed-in seating area with leather couches and arm chairs where people could wait for their guests to arrive. Because it was so late, most of the room was empty. Set along the back wall was a small coffee bistro that generated an appetizing smell throughout the area. I walked in that direction, while Brandon took a seat along the front glass wall.

Even though it was summer, and the temperatures hovered around 85 even this late into the night, I needed something to warm my stressed body. After ordering a caramel mocha with extra cream, I joined my brother on a small sofa. He didn't ask why I chose coffee in summer, he just smiled and patted my arm as I draped it across the back cushion.

"What do you think she'll say when she sees me with you?"

"She'll probably cry and not say anything."

Then he nodded deeply. "Yes! Remember that time we celebrated her 45th birthday. We pooled our money, earned over a year, to buy her tulips and Chinese takeout, oh and root beer floats. All of her favorite things."

"Speechless. I tell you. It's her go-to thing!"

I remembered Dad not being able to be there for her birthday. We wanted it to be a special one, not just because the year it marked but also because he wouldn't be there to celebrate with her. Instead of reminding him, I took a deep drag from my paper cup allowing the heat to sink deep into my stomach.

While we waited I told Brandon more about my relationship

with Will, how we met, and what led to our engagement and marriage. I told him more about Emmy, and he promised to be more involved in our lives. He had missed a lot of those precious moments and only understood the big picture of things—I found a guy, we got married, I became pregnant, and finally I had a daughter.

I could read the sadness in his face as I talked. What I saw in him was a slightly aged, more mature version of my brother. The big difference was that he was actually expressing interest in me and my life instead of just his life and the soccer team. I wondered if he thought he abandoned me, or that he should have stayed around for my needs.

"Dad and I were fine," I reassured him. "He's still the stubborn man he's always been. A tad boring for my liking, but I'm hoping to get him on a cruise soon. I've been working with Maggie on that one."

"That would be awesome, and wouldn't it be fun to do it as a family. Maybe in a year or so after Cass and I get settled into the whole marriage thing."

"I think you're pretty much already settled. Only thing you'll need to do is frame the paper that says you're legal now and put away all of the small appliances you'll get as gifts."

"What kind of small appliances are we talking here? I'm not looking for anything more than a blender and electric knife. Oh, and maybe a cocktail shaker," he said.

"I see what you did there—margaritas."

Brandon chucked, and I stopped mid-laugh, looking past him. A tall red-headed woman caught my attention. She wasn't a red head when she left, but her happy, deep-blue eyes and naturally rose-colored cheeks were features I'd not ever forget.

Mom had arrived.

Chapter 45

I hugged her. No words were necessary at that moment, but the arms I offered told her how much I missed her, and I held on for a few more seconds. When she saw Brandon tears that were building ran over and flowed freely down her cheeks. He joined in the embrace, and we stood like that in the middle of the walkway for a while.

Those people who disembarked the same plane had to walk around us. We didn't take the time to move, and eventually Mom broke the hug and stood back looking her two grown children in the face as if they were just born and laid upon her chest for the first time.

Nothing had changed.

She still held love for us as if she never left. We turned toward the baggage claim, and I walked with my mom at my side, my arm around her waist. Brandon led the way toward the escalator. It was then that he turned and asked how her flight was. While we waited for her luggage to make its way on the conveyor belt, we talked about Knoxville and her job. She was quick with her answers as if giving more details would reveal happiness we didn't think she deserved. I hoped that would change the more we got to visit with each other that weekend.

On the way to the airport we had passed an all-night diner. Now, on our way back to the hotel, I pulled in without asking my copilots if they'd like to stop.

"You read my mind," Brandon said.

"Me too. I'm starving. I haven't eaten since a late lunch at work," Mom agreed.

"And I haven't had a good diner milkshake in years."

Mom smiled at me. "Chocolate was always your favorite."

"With extra whipped cream," I added.

As we ate greasy hamburgers and ketchup-smothered fries washed down with milkshakes, we talked more about each of our lives. I learned more about what Mom did as a nurse in the pediatric wing of the hospital, and she was amazed at how much the Hope and Wellness center had done for people in our community. Both of us were introduced to a softer, happier side of Brandon, who would be married within a few hours to the true love of his life.

When it was time to leave, I was happy. I was happy to get this moment to talk with my mom and my brother. I was happy that each one of them was happy too. I didn't want to think how differently the night could have gone if there was tension or despair from any of us. But there wasn't. We laughed, shared things from our past that might have been forgotten, and most importantly addressed what happened with Mom and Dad.

"It's okay. I don't need to know the details of everything that happened. I understand that you were hurt. That you both were. But we are okay. All of us. We made it through everything, and we're stronger than most people probably imagined we could be. I love you guys. This moment, right here—at this lonely diner with some pretty awesome chocolate shakes—this is one memory I don't think will ever be topped. I got my family back."

Mom gave me a silent, sad hug from beside me on the booth. She was crying again. Brandon smiled shyly from across the table. To liven the mood, he threw his wadded straw paper into my hair. "I love you, Sis," he said.

Chapter 46

*F*inally making it back to the hotel room, I found Will watching TV on the lowest audible volume setting while Emmy was sleeping curled up in a ball beside him on the bed. The only light in the room was from the bathroom. Before approaching the bed to give him a kiss I deposited my purse onto the entry table where the bathroom light shone a bright beam onto the wooden surface. The envelope from Cassidy fell out as I untangled the straps from my arm, and I picked it up on my way to the bed where they both lay. "Mom made it in safely, and I deposited her in the lobby."

He eyed me for more details, smiling at my comment.

"You know what I mean. And we had a good chat." I bent over and kissed his forehead. Then I leaned further and kissed Emmy too.

I didn't tell him about talking with Brandon. He may have assumed that we visited with each other after he left to come back to the room, but I would save the details for the following day. It would require more hours that I had in me. "I'm taking a quick shower, and I'll be back in here in a few minutes."

I took the pajamas I laid out and my envelope from Cassie to the bathroom. As I ran the water to get it extra hot, I opened up my card. It was actually an invitation. It was for a bridal brunch tomorrow. Along with the traditional details an invitation contained, Cassidy handwrote a note to me at the bottom of the card. It read, *Can't wait for you to become my newest sister!* She signed her name with *hugs and kisses.* That was very sweet of her. Having three other real sisters, as well as six from the sorority house she was a member of in college it was nice that she wanted to include me in the same circles.

Before leaving, Brandon gave a similar envelope to our mom. She must have been invited too. I was happy I'd be able to spend more time with her, and that I would not be alone with Cassidy and the team of debutante girls she brought with her as her wedding party.

The warm spray of the shower penetrated to my scalp. I had turned the water on as hot as I could stand it, and the room was already fogging. In addition to the hot coffee from earlier, this was exactly what I needed to feel relief from the stressful day. Starting tomorrow, our family vacation would officially begin, and we would be able to enjoy the beach. It would be Emmy's first time seeing the ocean, and it had been at least six years since I was at the beach. Back then it had been for a quick spring break trip during college, and the four of us girls who came only had enough money for one night in a hotel, and it was two blocks from the beach.

Thinking about it now, we hadn't had a family vacation longer than a long weekend since before Emmy was born. The center kept Will and me busy, and anything else we did was with our daughter. Yes, this vacation was exactly what we all needed.

Chapter 47

I slept hard. I awoke at 8:30 to a small hand caressing my face. When I opened my eyes Emmy smiled and burst into laughter. Then she bounced on her knees to arouse me and started chanting, "Breakfast, breakfast, breakfast."

"How about we go get some breakfast and bring it up for mommy to eat in bed," Will suggested, removing Emmy from the bed to stop the bouncing.

I stopped him before she got too excited. "I wish I could. I have a bridal brunch with Cassidy in about an hour and a half. I will take coffee though."

One eyebrow perked on Will's face. "Bridal brunch, huh?"

I nodded and sighed while showing my surprise as well.

"Okay, Emmy. You heard the lady. We need to get her some coffee, stat."

"And a waffle. For me," she added.

"Yes, a waffle for you."

As they walked out of the door, she was telling her daddy how she had to have chocolate chips *and* syrup, not one or the other. He was nodding along in agreement and surely praying they didn't have chocolate chips as an option for toppings on the breakfast bar.

After they left, I took my time getting ready. I knew I'd be doing it all over again for the wedding that night but I felt the need to curl my hair, to take a few minutes to use all the brushes and applicators that came with the extra makeup I brought.

When I was done I felt beautiful. I smiled. I tried to remember back to when I was younger, and I didn't feel like that. I know it was part of me. I tell the story so often you'd think I'd rip the wound open. But I never did. I am completely healed, and having my parents and brother in the same place, again, after all these years has made my heart grateful as well. This is how true restoration must feel.

Mom smiled and motioned from across the room.

"Man, I feel out of place," I said as I slid into the stool across from her.

"You shouldn't. You look absolutely beautiful." Mom patted my hand.

"Thank you." I smiled.

"And how do you think I feel? I'm the mom who disappeared," she whispered in my direction.

I put my hand over hers and rubbed it lightly for reassurance. "Guess it's just you and me together at the misfits table then, huh?"

As expected, Cassidy spent all of three minutes talking to Mom and me. She promised to swing back around but never did. When everyone was leaving, the bridal party was shuffling her to the salon to get her hair done, so we were left with a wave goodbye in each other's direction. I mouthed *good luck* and she nodded a *thank you* in return.

"Well, I promised Emmy we'd make a sand castle, and that we could look for mermaids. Would you like to join us at the beach? Maybe I can even convince her to bury you in the sand?" I asked Mom.

"That sounds very appealing, almost even entertaining, but I think I'm going to track down my son. I have a lot to catch up with him about. Have fun at the beach though. I'll see you sometime later. I have a little girl to love on."

"See you soon, Mom."

Chapter 48

We ordered takeout sandwiches from the hotel deli and hit the beach about one o'clock. I knew the sun would chase us away before long, and I spent most of the time under the umbrella in a floppy hat and oversized glasses. I slathered myself and my family in SPF 50 sunscreen and sent them to the water's edge while I paged through a magazine. Every so often I'd zoom my camera to capture the perfect image of Will and Emmy making a sand castle or jumping through the surf.

There was a perfect, light breeze, and eventually the sound of waves lulled me into relaxation.

Before I knew it my dad was shaking me with his foot 45 minutes later. "Are you sleeping?"

"If I was I'm not now." I sat up and closed the magazine.

Emmy and Will were dragging a ditch from the water's edge to their castle to fill their moat. I waved them over and invited Dad to sit beside me.

"Take a break from the sun." I encouraged them all to join me under the large umbrella and passed out water bottles from the ice-filled cooler.

I straightened the beach towels, shaking them first to remove the sand that embedded its way into the threads. Dad was first to sit, staying mostly in the sun. "I need my vitamin D," he said.

"Where's Maggie?" I asked.

He pointed to a tiki hut. "Getting a drink." Before I could say anything he spoke again. "She likes drinks with umbrellas when she's at the beach. Doesn't want alcohol—just the umbrella."

"Oh, okay." I nodded.

After a few seconds, I asked, "So did you see her?"

"Yeah, she's still over there." Dad pointed.

"I mean Mom. Did you see Mom?"

Dad checked to make sure Maggie wasn't near. She was just turning our way with what could have been a lemonade with a large umbrella decorated the edge.

"Yeah, I saw her. We didn't talk and I didn't know if… you know with Maggie… could be awkward."

"Dad. You're adults. Divorced. Living in separate states. She's not going to be jealous."

He looked as if weighing options, not that I gave him any. "Mmm… Maybe. I don't know. If I get the chance, I guess I'll say hello."

"Okay. Well, there's your chance." I pointed with my head down the beach behind him. "She's coming this way."

Chapter 49

*T*he wedding had been beautiful. The tropical flowers and flowing ivory lace dresses were perfect against the ocean backdrop. Just a few rows of white folded chairs had been lined in a semicircle on the beach with a smooth sand aisle leading to the ivy and flower garland decorated archway. It was all simplistic in the most perfect way.

There were almost as many people in the wedding party as there were total guests. Seven attendants were on each side of the couple, and two very small children played in the sand at the bride's feet. They were twins, Ashlyn and Avery, Cassidy's niece and nephew. They were also failing at their jobs as flower girl and ring bearer. At two years old they weren't expected to be anything but cute, and I smiled as I watched them.

As low-key and simple as the wedding service was, the exact opposite was true for the reception. An outside beach front patio of the hotel was turned into a brightly colored picture of tropical paradise. Lights were strung around; a reggae band performed on a low-level stage to the side of an oversized dance floor.

For the possible 50 guests that were in attendance, the buffets around the dining area were more than the group could ever hope to tackle. As stuffed bellies danced the food off, Emmy passed out in my lap. I sat and watched the different groups around the room as each had their own fun. Some stayed on the dance floor without taking even a small break. Others stood around and visited as the alcohol was going down smoothly with each passing minute of conversation. This seemingly calm activity is probably what prompted the next chain of events.

Will was throwing away empty beer bottles from our table, none of which were ours. It was the pit stop he'd make on his way to the restroom. I was left at the table with a sleeping child in my arms. To my left were a group of bridesmaids surrounding a high bar table. There were three Ts in Cassidy's wedding party—Talia, Tiffany, and Tasha. One of the Ts tried to whisper, but just as one song died down and another started, there was a delay, and her voice carried a little louder than she would have liked. She was obviously responding to someone's question on who I was.

"She's Brandon's sister. The one who tried to kill herself in high school."

I looked up and met her eyes. I didn't know her. I didn't know any of the other Ts either. In fact, when Cassidy introduced them to me earlier in the day, it was as a whole, and I said *hello* and *nice to meet you* as a general greeting. So for any of them to know such personal information should have been upsetting. In fact, in the past, I would have reacted with one of two emotions—embarrassment or anger.

This time though I was neither. I was happy with who I have become. I knew my past is what made me better.

I smiled. When I did, she saw me. She was the one to be embarrassed.

Then I felt sorry for her.

Chapter 50

"We are not the wedding guests we used to be," Will said as he carried the sleeping bundle of child over his shoulder like a sack of potatoes.

I followed behind with the straps of my shoes laced around my first two fingers. My feet were killing me. Cute strappy shoes were not my favorite accessory. "I don't know if I was ever that kind of wedding guest." I checked my watch. 8:47.

Dancing had really just begun when we excused ourselves from the party. I was glad to have made it to the cake and to see my mom dance with Brandon. Everything after that would have to be relived through stories and videos.

It had been a long day. The beach alone can wear someone down, but with the emotions and adrenaline that coursed through my veins over the past couple days, I was ready for a vacation from the vacation. Yeah, the more I thought about it, the office did sound inviting right about now. At least it sounded normal. We'd have a few more days to relax alone as Mom and Dad would be heading to their respective homes tomorrow.

After putting Emmy to bed, we each took turns in the bathroom; showers and brushing teeth in silence so as not to wake her up. As I was applying some lotion, Will came up behind me and hugged me, planting a kiss on my neck.

"I love you. I'm happy you got to see everyone. That was nice."

"It was, wasn't it?" I turned around and embraced him, laying my head on his chest, "I can't wait to see how the future goes now."

"Might be bumpy."

"Might. Actually, I'd be surprised if it wasn't." I laughed. "I'm a pretty tough person now, though. I'm going to be able to handle it."

"Oh, no doubt." This time Will laughed.

I looked up and kissed him, then whispered, "More than you know."

Chapter 51

*B*randon and Cassidy's flight for their honeymoon was scheduled to leave around lunchtime the next day. Before heading to the airport, though, they invited Will, Emmy, and me along with Mom and Dad and Maggie to breakfast. It was nice having the family together. There were still moments of awkward silence and uncomfortable looks, but they were growing fewer and shorter as the trip had gone on. We told stories of the past and made plans to see each other in the future. There seemed to be an air of closure among the conversations.

Maggie and Dad left right after breakfast, and the newlyweds followed shortly after. I told Dad I'd be there to check on him by the weekend, and Maggie promised to keep him in line. I bid final congratulations to my brother and new sister-in-law. Cassidy was still embarrassed over how her bridal party spoke to me, and after apologizing over and over she finally knew I held no hard feelings toward her or any of the girls. It was an issue she'd have to deal with regarding her friends at a later date. My hug with her was longer than usual, so she'd feel reassured.

Mom thought about taking a few more days off from work to stay with us, riding back home with us and flying out of Greensboro at the end of the week. But, as a nurse her schedule had her coming in at 7:00 that night, and she didn't want to burden a fill-in to come in on her behalf.

"No time to even do laundry," she had noted. "But I promise to come stay on my next long weekend off work." She had pure excitement in her eyes, and seeing Emmy for the first time made her realize how much she really had missed. "I'm sorry I was so stubborn," she said as she hugged me goodbye. "It was my loss. I regret it, but this girl is stuck with me now." She tousled Emmy's hair, and Emmy hid in my shoulder.

"I love you, Mom. I'm happy we had this time together."

"It was so late. I should have done it sooner."

"Late's always better than never. At least it happened." I hugged her one last time, and Emmy turned and did the same.

With one last wink from Mom, we smiled and waved at each other.

Chapter 52

We rode in silence on the trip home later that week. My thoughts went back to the day at the school, when I met Des. He was on my mind a lot lately, and I felt that it was time to tell Will about everything that happened that day.

I turned down the radio which caught his attention.

"What is it, Hon?"

"I'm ready to talk about Des."

He looked at me briefly before staring back at the road ahead. "Okay, I'm all ears."

I looked back at Emmy who had fallen asleep a few miles down the road. She was still out like a light.

Then I started. "I was scared. More scared than I ever have been in my life. And it was a level of scared that I never thought I'd ever experience. There were so many times when my adrenaline was up, and my heart raced. It was like I was on a never-ending roller coaster. No wonder I slept for two days."

"Well, surgery on your ankle didn't help either."

I winced remembering the pain I endured that day even though my fibula was fractured. It still ached on a cool evening as a continual reminder of that day.

"I couldn't understand why they wouldn't tell me anything about what happened to Des. I didn't know the investigation that was going on and how Detective Michaels wasn't able to say anything until he was conscious again."

"Did you even know if he survived until they talked to you?"

"Not really. I overheard the nurse talking to the patrolmen that would come in. Most of the time they stepped out of the room, but once I heard her say, *he's improving.* I smiled believing he would be okay."

"But you didn't know."

"No. I hoped. I prayed. I had to see him. I had to talk to him. And I knew he'd want to talk to me to. Allison helped track him down for me. His aunt confirmed he was on probation but he wasn't ready to talk to anyone just yet. And that's okay. I knew he was going to be fine."

We rode a little further in silence. I was about to tell him how I also prayed to see Emmy and him again when he spoke first. "I remember when I heard about the shooting. It was the breaking news headline that came across on my work email. Before I even saw the school I knew it was you. Thank goodness I wasn't in a call because I dropped everything and ran to the car. I didn't even tell anyone I was gone until after I knew you were okay. And I prayed the entire way there. Well—I cursed the car for not going faster and traffic for being in my way—but between all that I prayed for your safety.

"And I prayed to see you guys again. I think it's the only thing that kept me from breaking down—thinking of you guys."

"But I guess it's a good time to confess something. I did something else I'm ashamed about," he admitted.

I looked at him to continue.

"I cursed God that he put you in that place when all that violence was happening. I asked *why you* so many times,—with every tear I was desperate to understand why it had to be *that* school, *that* day; any school of course was terrible but *that* one where you were. I was upset with God."

Before he finished, I was crying. I again looked at him. "I have never thought that way. I see why you were angry and why you questioned God. But I didn't see it that way."

"Why wouldn't you?" He glanced in my direction, and I could tell he was surprised with my answer.

"Because I was where that same God you curse needed me. I was where Des needed me. God put me in that school where I was needed to do His work at that moment."

And I immediately thought to the traffic I had been stuck in that day how I had to throw my purse into a drawer into the office while rushing to be on time on stage. Usually my purse was with me back stage, but I had to track down Principal Martinelli to give him my introduction. I didn't have my phone on me when I needed it. I hurt my ankle so I had to crawl to the nearest room to hide. The same room where Des was; the room without a desk phone. We had time to talk, and I had time to find out who he was—as he did with me. I don't know if he would have shot himself but even if he didn't and had succeeded with the scissors, he might not have been found until it was too late.

By now I was not the only one crying. Will's cheeks were damp with tears. He didn't say anything but reached over and took my hand with his, squeezing it tightly, finally understanding everything that I knew about that day.

Chapter 53

*I*f I had known this was the last conversation that I'd have with my husband, I would have probably picked a different topic. Maybe not. But I would have at least told him how much I love him, that I always loved him. I would have explained that my love for him will last past eternity and into the life to come.

But I didn't get that chance. I guess he already knew that, and God used this time to give him a better gift, a deeper understanding of who I was as a person. He also got to realize that the anger he was holding toward God was unfounded and unnecessary. I had already spent years showing Will the love that I kept in my heart for him, but my voice to tell that story was chosen for just this moment in time.

Seconds after I finished my story about Des I took my husband's hand, kissed it lightly and whispered my love to Will into the warm skin. I turned my head and drifted off for a short nap. During that time that I slept I felt so peaceful and light. It was a comforting sleep, one where I was enveloped in warmth even as the air conditioning cooled us throughout the car. My heart was full, and my mind was free while I slept a dreamless rest. It was the only time I had ever felt so relaxed, almost to the point of crying for joy.

It should have been a sign of what was about to happen. Instead I relished the few minutes after I opened my eyes, remembering what I just experienced. It was unknown to me then, but I was focusing on what was to come.

Chapter 54

I didn't feel dead. I didn't feel anything. There was a lack of everything—time, sound, air, light. I didn't feel anything, see anything or know anything. I was at peace. Period.

What I do remember is that everything happened in slow motion. I heard that your life flashes before your eyes when you die, and I understand it more as if you are in real time, but everything around you slows down.

We were traveling down the highway. It was just before 7:00. We had been at the coast for an extended vacation after the wedding, but we needed to get home before the next morning. It would be Wednesday, and I had a meeting with a young mom-to-be in the morning. Will was to attend an off-site seminar on non-profit leadership.

Emmy was in the backseat singing and playing with a musical toy after waking from her nap. It was approaching sunset but more importantly after dinner time, especially hers. I asked her if she was hungry, and when she said *yes* I unbuckled my seatbelt ready to climb into the back to make her a snack. I assume it was the most ironic 4.6 seconds known to man. I started over the console just as the sun broke the surface of clouds blinding Will. At that moment, traffic in front of us came to an abrupt stand-still, and Will slammed on the brakes. We hit the back end of the semi. The driver of the big rig probably didn't even know we hit him. When the impact happened I focused on Emmy's face, saw her close her eyes, then I closed mine as the screeching turned to silence, and everything went dark, as if a light switch was shut off.

Chapter 55

$\mathcal{W}$ill understood what would happen after I passed away. He knew where I'd go and believed in what was waiting for me on the other side. When a person has such faith it's hard to be that upset. But then reality of *the now* sets in, and he realizes the things that he will miss about that person on earth.

He looked at our daughter and thought of the many years of memories that will be made alone, without her mom to share them with. The first day of kindergarten, the end of kindergarten and graduation in little blue gowns, the homecomings, proms, boyfriends, first day of college, more graduations, engagement and wedding, and eventually children of her own. And so he cried. He didn't want to do those things without me.

I wish I was able to send him a message, to tell him to not worry about that. I couldn't watch it happen as the activities play out, but one day I will hear from them when we're all together again. I wanted Will to know that I loved him with everything in my being. Every ounce of me was dedicated to him, and Emmy was the light of my light. I found love and kept it until the end—albeit be it my end—but I never missed out on that.

He would relish the little things—like using the same detergent and shampoo just to smell me again. Then he would be angry and sad and buy new soaps just to get the smell of me out of the house. In a few months the cycle would begin again, and the same laundry detergent that was my familiarity would be back on the shelf once again. He would do anything he could to keep me close.

For now, he concentrated on getting through the saddest day of his life.

"I honestly don't know what to say," Dave practically whispered to his son-in-law, catching his voice before cracking.

"I don't either. How does someone prepare for this?"

"You don't."

They talked for a while before the funeral officially began. As the pastor arrived and asked everyone to sit, Dave turned to leave and joined Maggie across the aisle, but Will stopped him remembering the Post-it in his pocket. He gave Dave the message that once hung in his wife's office, the one with the speech she said to her dad the night of graduation.

Chapter 56

*T*he service was private. Only family and a select few friends were present. Lily wouldn't have wanted a crowd or people to make a fuss on her behalf. She was a private person, and Will would respect that last wish of hers.

Looking around the room at her parents and brother, he could see them willing him to be strong, but their eyes remained sympathetic as well. The chapel that we were in was small, lights dim, and the air was almost painfully cool. Or maybe he was just chilled from continued disbelief. For that reason, he kept his suit jacket buttoned, even though it, along with the tie were suffocating him at the moment.

Their neighbors and coworkers sat toward the back, each one with eyes downcast and tissues ready at hand as needed. Allison dotted her eyes every few seconds, but the tissues seemed to be failing as she continually pulled new ones from a box on her lap. Will wished tears would come to him at that moment, but he was surprisingly numb. He chuckled to himself at the thought of Lily making him strong for the moment—just long enough to get through this. She always had that power over him. Why would today be any different?

After the pastor welcomed everyone, Lily's dad would be first to speak. Her mom would be next if able. For now, she held her eyes shut with tissues.

Dave echoed the pastor and thanked everyone for coming. As he said it though, he felt the words were odd considering the circumstance. Quickly changing direction, he held up the yellow Post-it.

"This small piece of paper changed my life twice. I never thought

I'd see it more than once let alone today as well. The first time was a time of desperation. The next was of inspiration. I'm going to use it now for confirmation."

He flipped the paper back and forward for everyone to see, then continued. "Each side has 27 words. They are 27 meaning-filled words. What I have to say or how I feel however can't be summed up in only 27 words. So I won't.

"I was not always best for Lily. But she was best for me. She was best for a lot of people, and she brought the best out of a lot of people. I think that's probably what she did for me too. I know it's what she did for all of you. When she was born, I was blessed. When her life was spared a decade ago, I was blessed. And finally as I tell her goodbye and until we meet again, I am blessed. She made me a better person, and I was loved. I hope she knew that I loved her too and that she could feel just a fraction of that love, because even in those times when I wasn't the best dad, I still loved her. And yes, Lily, I even *liked* you. And was proud of you—proud of her."

Toward the end he felt like he mumbled. He hoped if she was not in any way able to hear him, she heard his plea. He pocketed the note and stepped from the podium.

As Dave returned to his seat, he looked over at Sharon. She shook her head, and her face told him that she was not ready. She slammed her eyes shut and dropped her jaw. She didn't even know if she could stand. She most certainly knew she couldn't speak.

Dave nodded instead toward Will, and he stood and quietly passed him on his way to the pulpit. His suit, that he once filled out perfectly now hung from his frame as he'd visibly lost some weight. He looked back at his parents. His mom couldn't even look at him as she quietly cried into a tissue. His dad, looking defeated, entertained a playful and unaware Emmy on his lap.

As Will began to talk his voice cracked from emotion, and he took a moment to clear his throat and gather strength. "I've been to a funeral before where the pastor talked about the hyphen, the dash between the person's birth year and death year and how it's what means the most, more than the years listed. Lily's hyphen was only just beginning. It didn't even get to be more that a dot for her... for us."

He swallowed loudly and forced himself to go on. "I realize now that even though she didn't have long on this earth she saved more people, helped more people that probably someone with the longest hyphen ever could in his or her lifetime. The calls she took at the center, the speeches she gave… the people she met," he thought of Des, then continued, "they were her dash. The world will always be a better place because she lived in it. Now, her work will continue in another place. I wanna believe the Lord saw her greatness, and now she's training angels to do their jobs. So it's okay that she's in that place. And one day we'll be together again. Until then I'm gonna live my life, and raise our daughter to be as great as her mother was, so we can get there too."

"When we see each other again she won't have pain from her past, and I won't have pain from the future I face without her."

He bit his lip and finished with his final goodbye. "Lily, I love you—more than you know."

His mom met him as he walked back to the front row. She hugged him for a long time, and the room was anything but silent as weeping and sniffling filled every being that was there. It was heartbreaking. It was devastating. And it was undeniable truth.

Brandon was the last to speak that day. "Her hyphen may have just begun, as Will said, but she didn't leave anything undone. Most families feel strain at times, but I think she didn't feel any of that. What was broken was repaired. What may have been hopeless once was thriving now. What she did for so many others came back to her ten-fold. And she deserved it all. I will miss her. I will always, until the day I see her again, wish for another conversation or visit with her."

As if he was a machine that took change to operate, and the money was all spent, he ran out of words and just fell silent. Then, he turned and walked back to his seat with a pool of tears ready to fall.

Chapter 57

When Will drove past the Hope and Wellness Center after the service, there were crowds of people walking along the sidewalk. He quickly recognized the people who worked for or volunteered at the center. In addition, there were some old neighbors they had once lived near and people that had walked through the doors of Hope and Wellness seeking help or guidance. Some stood and watched him as he drove by. All smiled sadly and nodded in his direction. Most surprising however, were the people he just met a few months ago.

The most people that lined that street watching his approach were from the newest church Lily found. They were her Christian family, their family in Christ. Will slowed to a stop in the middle of the road and hung his head as tears fell. She was baptized just seven months ago into that church, and now here they all stood. They came to say goodbye to their new friend.

Will looked up and sighed. Brilliant light emulated from the front of the building as if a UFO was shining its beam down to the ground. When he got closer, he saw what caused the light. There were hundreds of lit candles along with an array of gifts and flowers lining the sidewalk and front steps. The impact she made in people's lives were on display for everyone to see, and her light was still shining for all to cherish.

Epilogue

$\mathcal{I}$t will take years and many visits to Lily's grave-
side to realize the coincidence that lies before her
family's eyes. They will lay wreaths at Christmas,
flowers on her birthday, and drawings made by
Emmy with each visit. They will weep silently as
they stare are her name, engraved with precision
over dates that show she was too young to die.
Something will one day catch her father's eye as he visits her on
what should have been her 30th birthday. The message engraved
under those dates reads:

YOU WILL ALWAYS BE OUR DAUGHTER, OUR SISTER,
A LOVING MOTHER, AND A BEAUTIFUL WIFE.
BUT NOW YOU ARE ALSO OUR ANGEL.
FLY HIGH DEAR LILY GIRL!

27 Words.

About the Author

*K*L Palmer calls herself *the working mother's author.*

Even though she hasn't (yet) written a book on how to be a better mom, or how to incorporate your personal life into your long work day; she did follow her dream and write a novel—or five. She hopes to inspire other working moms to write, or follow their dreams wherever they lead, and not give up.

One thing that sets her apart from others is her propensity to write what she calls *break chapters*—chapters short enough to take a bathroom break, commercial break, or smoke break away from life, with each averaging just two to three pages. She wants to bring reading back into the lives of busy people; to show that you can, in fact, enjoy a book and take time for yourself; and do so with the limited and precious spare time you have.

Born and raised in a quiet Amish-surrounded community in Pennsylvania, she now resides in Tennessee with her family. In addition to being employed full time in a corporate real estate position, Palmer remains passionate about her church and her writing. She jokes that her mind never shuts off. Even in the most inopportune time she's jotting down ideas for the next manuscript.

Just don't tell her boss!

Acknowledgment

I want to send a special "Thank You" to my good friend Jenn. She was my impromptu content editor for this book. It was her voluntary duty to keep my characters complete and storyline flowing smoothly, and she did it very well!

Lily is a character that has a loving dad there beside her throughout her entire life, but it isn't until she becomes an adult when she realizes how strong the bond truly is between a father and daughter. The same is true for me. I sadly learned this when I moved away. I wish we could be closer in distance, but I know we'll remain close in our hearts forever.

I love you Dad.

9 781957 344355